HOW PALE THE WINTER HAS MADE US

Adam Scovell

Influx Press
London

Published by Influx Press
The Greenhouse
49 Green Lanes, London, N16 9BU
www.influxpress.com / @InfluxPress
All rights reserved.
© Adam Scovell, 2020

First edition 2020. Printed and bound in the UK by TJ International.

Paperback ISBN: 9781910312452
Ebook ISBN: 9781910312469

Editor: Gary Budden
Copyeditor: Momus Editorial
Proofreader: Trudi Suzanne Shaw
Cover design: Vince Haig
Interior design: Vince Haig

For Caroline

'… I am a voluntary exile, a wanderer by design, unwise with a purpose, everywhere a stranger and everywhere at home, letting my life run its course where it will, rather than trying to guide it, since, in any case, I don't know where it will lead me.'

— Goethe, *Italian Journey*

Strasbourg.

1

It was on an autumn day in Strasbourg when I first saw the Erl-King. I had not somehow crossed into another world in a moment of lax attention or dreamed the veiled figure into shadowy existence from my window. Instead, I was witnessing a genuine apparition on account of the news I had just received concerning my father's suicide back in Crystal Palace. The trees, still memory-blind, had once more thrown off their leaves and the ground was amber with their dead. I can recall how I first found out about his – that is, my father's – death, even if the words 'Your father has taken his own life' seemed impossible to imagine in any written form, never mind on the small, digital screen of my phone. But, suffice to say, the feeling it left me with was that I was now dead too, sharing in his action so to speak, as the Erl-King came for both our souls. I was near Place Gutenberg at the time, sitting in a cafe reading and writing as I had done regularly throughout the summer, enjoyably in the epicentre of the city watching its streets breathe with people. On receiving this news, my phone flaring up like an accursed beacon, I had been possessed by the unusual urge to strike at my own eyes, to slash my pupils and remove the potential of having to see our world again – a world which I knew my father, whom I had admittedly hated, to have departed from. Alongside this violent sensation, I felt a numbing delirium that, in my new state, I assumed resembled the slight few moments just after the heart had finally stopped beating, the blood slowing to a bare minimum before halting entirely and the world fading to a lasting crimson sleep. It was then that the black shroud of the Erl-King had drifted past the window, though only I noticed its shadowy movement.

Strasbourg lay all around me, familiar streets with cobbles, old buildings constructed in a mixture of styles, most of them incredibly preserved considering the many conflicts that had befallen the city over the years. My eyes, yet to be slashed in dismay, stared out of the window at the small groups of wandering tourists, who were thankfully blind to the Erl-King. I had found myself staring aimlessly with ease before I had received the burdensome news regarding my father, but now all windows possessed the potential for a black messenger to pass by, to intimidate and swallow the light. Images of my father's sodden body, hanging from a rope in Crystal Palace Park, bothered the corners of my eyes every few minutes like a disease. What were these tourists searching for? I recall thinking, as I thought I felt my father's legs brush against me before acknowledging it as nothing. Someone had stopped to take a picture of the cathedral which stood impressively and deliberately at the end of the small road. Perhaps the photo was to be looked at on some future occasion when, with all then lost in a lonely twilight year, delight would once more be encouraged by the image of a blurry building. I wanted images of this place too, or at least this place before the Erl-

King had roamed its streets, images taken before that moment when the words had appeared on my phone. Sometimes, like a terrible dream that lingered on awakening, I felt the essence of his death still around me like a silver mist. I batted away his hanging feet and legs from behind my shoulder, as if he had hanged himself, of his own accord, directly and permanently above me. I wished my mother, acidic and angry, hadn't written the details of his death so casually; that second text did not need the detail of my father's hanging, and not least in the detail of its location which brought to mind nothing less than those cartoonish figures of dinosaurs from my childhood visits. It was deliberate on my mother's part, for we had what could be called an abrasive relationship. Of course she would want to plague me with images of my father's hanging body, instead of a much simpler abstract death, suitable for a painter. Perhaps he had committed such an action so he could keep watch over his daughter, now sat in a Strasbourg cafe a long way from home and wondering what to do. The painter who, by all accounts, had failed to make any real success, had finally gone through with it and, in keeping with his history, had made more work to return home to.

I had been in the city for some weeks visiting my partner. He was now away travelling for several months around South America, and had already been gone for a few days when I received the news about my father. Occupying his flat in the Petite France area of the city, I was due to leave once more for England in his absence, back to the university and the emptiness of academic life, albeit in a new position acquired through several months of tedious labour and interviews. Accompanying him to the station earlier in the week to wish him farewell, I had wished deeply for him not to go, but also to be able to stay in his flat rather than return to England, which seemed to me to be sinking that autumn. 'You know you can stay if you really want to,' he wrote in a message before his flight. It was the sort of open-ended message I had grown used to, his inability to commit to even the smallest of things being his one true character trait, a consistency of subversion. Even if he had vehemently wanted me to leave, this would have been the same message sent, the same insinuation as to his true meaning. The flat was, after all, empty, and I still had some money left over to pay for the costs of running it in his absence, so there would be no trouble on his part. In hindsight, it was a blessing that he left before I heard the news of my father's demise, imagining the coy, softly-spoken words of comfort that would have subsumed us all in an awkward glaze. He could never *do* sincerity without a sickly sense of tenderness. I could not have conveyed or explained to him my behaviour that was to follow in those winter months either, his mind being logical; a cold logic that meant he was constantly wrong but simultaneously and technically right. England was impossible for me now that I knew what would face me on my return, and his beautifully empty flat was irresistible. More than any natural sense of dismay from returning home, as on previous trips, there would now be the addition of a weight of paperwork and the responsibilities that come with any death. I would not return to England then, no matter how much my scheming mother pleaded via texts and online messages. Her very words had been augmented by the habit of discussing everything through such technology. I imagined her posting about my father's death with an added 'Like and share if you agree'. Strasbourg was to be my island upon which to explore and seek refuge; to lose myself in the arms of the Erl-King. Anything to avoid the responsibility of such paperwork. I did not, however, know or decide any of this when I was sat in the cafe near Place Gutenberg, when my harridan mother had messaged about my father's death. I felt little else in that moment, just a sense of drowning, a desire to blind myself to this world, to follow that shroud around the corner beyond the square. That is why I began to walk. My father's veins were blackened for a time with a virulent greed for success, I thought, a perfect victim for the stealer of infancy, the stalker now of my dreams.

It was only when wandering out of this cafe later, after a further two cups of strong, bitter coffee which made my hands and knees shake, that the idea occurred to me; to, at the very least, not answer phone calls from England and to keep the news a secret from my partner now that he was on his travels. The idea to stay in the city, and in some sense *map it*, came later in the week. I was not to take my flight back to Stansted Airport from Strasbourg-Entzheim, or return to the university until, so I told myself, I had mapped the centre of Strasbourg, traversed the very epicentre of city, the Grande Île, turned into an island by the Ill – the tributary of the Rhine – and its water flowing to the east through the Canal du Faux-Rempart. Perhaps it was the Erl-King guiding my hands, or simply the current of the water which I felt unable to cross. I did not come upon this plan alone but by chance thanks to a stranger whom I spoke to later when wandering. I could not walk far in my dazed state for, as anyone who has been grief-stricken will be acutely aware, the body briefly forgets almost all of its basic functions and distinctions. There was no sign of

the shroud that had presented itself when first hearing of
my father's death. Death renders the vision heavy, hence
my desire to obliterate my sight, preventing new thoughts
from spreading. But my sight was also two-tiered, seeing
the shadow-world of history beyond the present under
which a sepia placidity lay. I was at that moment near the
cathedral that lay at the heart of the city, its stone designs
staring out over the other buildings and towards me like a
great mountain. I stared back, meandering forwards in one
sense but totally directionless in another.

Is there such a thing as a destination after a father's
suicide? Is not all direction briefly lost when a parent, even
one so loathed and ambivalent, is finally silenced? And
yet, even in the haze of the news which descended quickly
and sharply, each step had hidden within it some *potential*,
as if I was about to walk into the ground, into a Dantean
underworld. England was far in the distance, in its own
manic silence, slipping beyond the waves. Strasbourg was,
on the other hand, firm, and away from the home that was
once mine, long since soured. I was in luck for distractions
that day as, in spite of feeling totally alone, except for the Erl-
King of course, the main road of Rue du Vieux-Marché-aux-
Poissons had its weekly fair of antiques and was therefore
bustling with people, all alive and well and not plagued
by shrouds. The street was lined with a huge variety of
tents and tables, some specialising in specific items such
as records or books but the majority contained a pleasing
mixture of old objects with no discernible theme other than
age. There were boxes of photographs, old crockery, swords,
piles of unusual manuscripts, wooden objects whose use
was impossible to discern, keys to unknown doors and an

endless array of similarly mysterious things. One vendor took the time to show me a complex padlock built in India which required several cunning manoeuvres before finally unlocking its overhanging strip of metal bar. My mind wandered as methodically and as slowly as my legs while I smoked a cigarette, my own being dissolving pleasantly into each array of items, blocking thoughts of my father as I approached each table. I would not cry for him. An older man, who, after a later conversation, I found out to be a regular of the stalls called Monsieur Breon, was arguing loudly with the owner of one of the tables with its back to a small square. I saw that he was haggling down the price of a golden pocket watch he had taken a fancy to. At that point, however, the French rolled so aggressively and precisely from his mouth that it was not too difficult to imagine that he was confronting a man who had been involved in romantic dalliances with his wife, or had perhaps stolen some land from him just like in the book by Zola that I had, until that day, been working my way through during my stay. The table I had stopped to look at was filled with interesting objects and, in those minutes, I felt my worries flitter away into the air with the smoke I exhaled as each thing was closely observed and handled. My body was on Rue du Vieux-Marché-aux-Poissons – a road that was to prove pivotal, as if it were the main vein to the heart of the city and my growing interest in it – but my eyes, far from staring up at the hanging body of my father in Crystal Palace, were looking at a miniature landscape built from paraphernalia of all sorts. This world was constructed from objects and knick-knacks fallen from a flowing slipstream of time and had gathered on the shoreline of those tables.

The man that the troublemaker, Monsieur Breon, was arguing with was called Brice. He looked like an inversion of everything Monsieur Breon was. Whereas the arguing man was rotund, wearing extravagantly patterned clothes and adorned with an array of patchy facial hair, Brice was excessively thin with black glasses and yet exuded a warm presence rather than a cold and rigid persona sometimes associated with slim, older men. Both of the tables there belonged to him, and I admired them as he bargained about the watch. *'Non, c'est trop cher,'* Monsieur Breon repeated as a mantra, as if its repetition would somehow rectify the problem and Brice would give in. The watch, as I peered covertly over from my stance at the adjacent table, didn't seem particularly special. The gold had managed to attract some dark patches on the rear made from a variety of substances, its hands didn't seem to be moving at all and, by all accounts, it seemed a relatively redundant thing.

It was not to be Monsieur Breon's day. After a final shake of Brice's head, Monsieur Breon raised his hand, swiped it down in a gesture of theatrical nonchalance and walked slowly off, hands soon thrust deeply in his pockets, towards another table nearer the square of Place des Tripiers, which was entirely bordered with rows of tables selling trinkets and antiques. Brice spotted me and came over to ask if I needed help, first in French, I remember, before he realised from my dress sense that I was probably at the least *British* if not *English*. At that precise moment I did not need help, except in escaping the Erl-King. Only moments later, however, I spotted a photo half covered by a transparent paperweight filled with colourful shards of curved glass. It was as if the inside of the paperweight was liquid, devised by a mind whose perception was interrupted and haphazard. It was not, however, the paperweight but the photograph safeguarded underneath that intrigued me. Most of the other tables and stalls had boxes of old photographs too, but Brice's table had just this one, half hidden under the paperweight like a secret. It was an old picture, black and white when it was first produced but now rendered coffee-coloured by the passing of time. In the picture there sat a well-dressed man on a chair. It seemed unusual as the chair was clearly designed for indoor use and yet the picture was outside. The sitter had perhaps thought that it was a good idea for this portrait to be taken in the garden, and I imagined his pompous hassling of those around him as a chair was fetched from some great French house and sat on the grass of a large, expansive garden. The man was holding what could have been either a walking stick or a riding cane, his oversized hat giving the slight appearance of a cowboy out of place in the lost memories of Europe. He had a noticeable moustache and an unusual amount of skin before his ear decided to begin, seeming from the angle of the photograph as if it was attached at the last minute to the very rear of his skull in a moment of haste. The edge of the photo faded to a white border upon which there was some writing, composed in beautifully flowing black ink. It suggested '*Bonjour ma chère Mathilde! Charles*' as well as having the date upon it, running up the side as ivy crawls up walls. I felt slightly self-conscious asking Brice for information about the photograph, considering that I had only just declined his help a few seconds before, but the seller didn't seem to mind, especially as he could see the difficulty with which I slowly constructed my plea in French.

'It's a nice photograph,' he said in slow but excellent English, in what I assumed was an opening gambit to bargain for a sale higher than it was worth. I agreed with him, playing along in this slight farce, as I knew from the moment I saw the photograph that, no matter what price Brice asked, I was going to buy it. There was something alluring about the picture; it seemed from a different world, not only one from before the death of my father but also entirely before my father had in fact existed. I could, so I thought, see the man in the photograph walking around these same streets; fitting in perfectly with the architecture that still stood all around where the dead man's photo now sat being blown by the faint breeze on the stall. The friction, if such a ghostly rewalking could occur, would be from the multitude of shops, many of which were American, clashing their garish colours with this man's clothing. 'Four euros,' Brice said, unable to hide the slight tonality of hope from his bargain. To his surprise, I instantly accepted and drew a crumpled five euro note from my pocket. The swiftness of this action caused suspicion to rise briefly within the seller, who looked at the photograph again on both sides before accepting that he couldn't see anything of value in it and taking the money. I assumed, rightly as Brice soon told me, that he was checking for some rare stamp, perhaps adorned on the back, that he had missed. 'I wouldn't have spotted it anyway,' he said later.

'There's an interesting story with this man, though,' he suggested as he collected my change from a small tin box hidden behind a pile of ephemera. 'In fact, it actually has to do with that square up the road.' I was surprised by how smoothly his English flowed, reminding me of how attractive I had found the same careful attention to language in my own partner when I first met him. But I had become used to other people's proficiency with languages there, something mostly alien back home, and ashamed of my own lack of fluency. We began to talk, or at least Brice began to talk, and I took great comfort in his voice and the story that it slowly unwound. *Even your voice is insufferable, Isabelle, your father deserved better than you: we both did.* Mere minutes before, I could think of nothing else in the world than my father's body hanging from a tree in Crystal Palace Park and the hovering Erl-King roaming in search of souls, my soul perhaps. Now I was transported, feeling closer to the streets of Strasbourg, more so than I had in my previous weeks here, even with my partner who hated having to leave the flat when not called out to the hospital for his internships in its various departments.

Brice continued his story, sometimes pausing to find a paper cup of coffee which must have turned cold with the insistent autumn breeze blowing through the streets. 'The man in the photo,' he said, 'is Monsieur Jacques Cail, sat in his garden at the turn of the century. I'm not particularly fond of photographs – only a fool tries to make any money from them on these stalls – but I came across this picture of Jacques a while ago and thought it would draw someone's attention. You've proved me, err, correct…' He stopped. 'Isabelle,' I said, filling in the gap that his pause had quietly asked me to close. 'Isabelle! Well, you've proved me right Isabelle. There is something that draws the eye, don't you think? Jacques lived not far from here for a time, in a spectacular apartment on Rue de la Nuée-Bleue. Before that he lived in the countryside in a big house just outside the city. It's funny really,' he continued, 'all that wealth and here he is, just a photograph.' Brice could tell that I was interested in his story, not least from the intensity with which I looked at him during his little speech. I stared often with this intensity after that day, noticing people averting their gaze when meeting mine, as if I had become possessed. Taking the photograph, I asked, 'What is the connection to the square? Do you mean Place des Tripiers here?' I said this while making a motion with my head to indicate the direction, noticing the unusual bronze statue hidden in between the stalls. 'Oh no!' he exclaimed. 'Place Gutenberg. Jacques' history is connected with Gutenberg, as a matter of fact.' If I had not already paid for the photograph of Monsieur Jacques Cail, I would have assumed that Brice was making up some extravagant story using the history of the city to make a few extra euros on a slow market day. But there was no reason for him to lie and so I let him continue, although he had already paused of his own accord. I considered the likelihood of this apparent connection to Johannes Gutenberg, the eminent goldsmith-turned-printer who began the print-publishing revolution of Europe in the 1400s. I half expected Brice to pull out one of Gutenberg's famously expensive Bibles and attempt some sort of sale for the – undoubtedly fake – item. Yet he seemed serious, persistently looking over my shoulder in between talking, as if he also sometimes saw things hanging there, or drifting into view. 'If you are really interested,' he said as his eyes steadied back towards mine, 'come back this time next week when the stalls are set-up and I'll tell you of Jacques Cail and Gutenberg. I think I may have some other photos to show you, if I can remember where I put them. No promises to sell them of course, as they're of more importance to me than that one there. But, still, let us speak next week.' That seemed an end to the matter for now and so, shaking Brice's hand, I left the old man to look after another approaching customer and took off back up the street with the intention of circling around via Grand'Rue, and eventually back to my partner's flat on Rue du Cygne in Petite France; a modern terracotta block sat behind the hospital and in front of the city's historic quarter.

Is this the cure, I remember thinking; the cure to the mourning of a hated loved one? Simply distraction? I barely felt any different from the minutes before I had heard the news of my father's suicide when sat in the cafe near the cathedral. Even potential tears had failed to arrive. It was through my naivety, of course, that I assumed mourning to be an instant injury rather than a slow illness that ravages silently, that changes your whole behaviour until it is too late to remedy when finally diagnosed. The Erl-King was not to be shaken off so easily. I did not perceive then that I had subtly moved onto a different psychological track, one that required the very metamorphosis of the self. To fill the mind with details of the past and match its sepia glare, of the passing of time lived by others; that seemed to me, after that morning's visit to Brice's stall, the plain and simple cure. I no longer had the urge or surreal feeling of the need to remove my sight, to slash my eyes to avoid the hanging corpse; my initial reaction to my father's death. My mother's blunt words, digital and ephemeral, had equally vanished into a pixelated realm of non-memory. I had a different desire to earlier: to know Strasbourg, to see more, rather than blind my eyes. Perhaps through this, and in spite of being a terrible daughter to the remaining relatives – especially my harridan mother, who I knew would be left to handle everything – I arrogantly felt I could face the death of that failed painter in Crystal Palace alone. I wandered past the stalls that lined the Rue du Vieux-Marché-aux-Poissons and back up to the main square, lighting another cigarette.

I had never paid particular attention to the square before, only noting its name and never making any real connection to Gutenberg himself. It was just a name, like that of my father etched onto the corner of canvases and now fading into oblivion through finitude. Many roads and squares are named after people in many different cities around the world, so it did not hold true that such places would have a genuine connection to the person, even if only in the form of a statue as in Place Gutenberg. Passage Walter Benjamin further into the city, for example, had no connection to Walter Benjamin that I could find and had, so a dated website told me, only been so named since 1994. It was far from the Spanish hotel in Portbou where the philosopher had died, the Parisian arcades where he had wandered or the house where he had been born in Berlin. But his name had travelled, carrying his quiet tragedy to a small passage in Strasbourg, more an alleyway really. My father's name would not travel, except into the ground as his paintings rotted and turned to compost in the garden on Gypsy Hill.

Though the buildings that made up Place Gutenberg were clearly incredibly old, most had a modern sheen to their ground floor sections. Many had extravagant clothing boutiques that clashed heavily with the architecture, showcasing expensive dresses, photographic blow-ups of models in a variety of different styles, and awkward mannequins in uncomfortable positions but still impeccably dressed. The thin bodies on display reminded me of my father; the lifeless but stylish figures causing a brief confusion, imagining his bones shining from a thinning corpse. But he soon faded as the square took a greater hold of my interest. I had walked it so many times already and yet had never really been *within it*. It had been a middle ground between destinations rather than somewhere to consider in itself. For the first time, I noticed the statue that dominated the huge area of pedestrianised walkway. I went towards it and realised, to my embarrassment, that the statue depicted Gutenberg himself, standing over the square, watching, and I had never noticed before. I later researched the statue, intrigued as to its qualities, possibly heightened by having simply ignored its presence in all my traversing through the square, either to the river, Grand'Rue or Place Kléber. The statue, so a researcher had written on a local blog, was installed in 1837, the same year that the architect, Gustave Klotz, became master of the cathedral and in charge of its restoration. Klotz is now commemorated in a monument just like Gutenberg, though, unlike Johannes, Klotz crouches underneath one of the pillars in the cathedral, still bearing its weight upon his back and working to maintain the building's state of grace even today.

Gutenberg's statue was made by the sculptor Pierre-Jean David d'Angers, the renowned French artist who, among other things, was responsible for several sculptures of the writer Honoré de Balzac, including the writer's bust that now sits with the gathering leaves upon his tomb in Père Lachaise Cemetery in Paris. I remembered dragging my partner to see Balzac's statue in another autumn; walking along the dark paths covered in the mushy remains of

fallen leaves, and trying desperately to ignore his boredom
at being in the cemetery, not helped by his hangover from
drinking overpriced Belgian beers the night before in
Belleville. He was going on about the future of coding,
how the statue would one day be recreated simply by
mathematical constructs, three-dimensional printers and
the like. His world, that is our world, killed uniqueness. I
had hated him then as we stood below Balzac's bust. Pierre-
Jean David d'Angers' figure of the goldsmith stood just as
confidently in Place Gutenberg, showcasing his invention to
the world along with his first Bible made from the printing
press. The whole figure was made of a dark material and
his small invention rested at his feet, the little structure
of wood and metal that would change the world with its
ability to spread thoughts and ideas far and wide. The plinth
was adorned with dramatic, busy renditions of the historical
events shaped by printed and documented paraphernalia.
One panel showed the signing of the American Declaration of
Independence, another showing many writers and thinkers
of Europe including John Milton, Jean-Jacques Rousseau and
a perturbed Immanuel Kant, who looked surprised, perhaps
at the realisation in hindsight that his skull was far larger
and wider than the average German's of his day, his eyes
threatening to pop out with the pressure. The most intriguing
panel, however, which took a few minutes to understand fully,
showed William Wilberforce freeing the slaves, possible at
last due to the documentation of the abolitionists. It was, so I
thought, a moot point considering the numerous bureaucratic
documentations that had allowed and aided the slave trade in
the first place. The meaning and interpretation of Gutenberg's
invention was infinite.

I must have seemed odd taking note of this statue in such detail as I noticed several people looking in my direction with a general unease. A fairground ride was situated just behind the statue, spinning around with twee music and housing a number of children riding plastic horses and fairy-tale coaches to nowhere. Perhaps I was meant to be watching the enjoyment of the children, just as several adults were doing. But as soon as I noticed this whirling presence, it began to grate and annoy. The music it produced sounded like a twinkly Strauss waltz and felt a bizarre accompaniment to the image of the freeing of slaves. Gutenberg seemed to be doing his utmost not to notice the strange, new presence of the merry-go-round, glaring straight towards the building of the Concorde Assurance, now occupied by a Société Générale bank, a Cyrllius clothes shop and a lingerie shop called Chantelle which lay directly in Gutenberg's eyeline. His modern view was to be the ever-changing collections of women's lingerie and negligee, turning the body into lavish patisseries. In one corner, so I researched, the Pfalz had stood; where the city's agency was conducted when it was still under its own rule. The building itself was demolished, I read later, but such was the city's nostalgia for its days of self-governance, especially during its turbulent history in subsequent years when it changed hands between nations bloodily and often, that a model of the building had been commissioned in 1895. Strasbourg's self-governance was finally taken away by Louis XIV, though it must be said that its ruling before this was conducted by a variety of large, powerful families and was far from democratic. Place Gutenberg itself was once named Place Saint-Martin, after the church and the prominent graveyard that had stood at

the centre and heart of the city. I would soon begin to buy
postcards of my various visits over that winter, including
one of Place Gutenberg. A shop opposite my partner's flat
specialised in old postcards and, as the images in sepia
seemed more accurately to express my hounded vision of
the places, I preferred them to the photographs on my phone
which were really *nothing*.

It was only when the music from the ride had ceased and
the several children upon it had meandered off dizzily into
the arms of impatient parents, that I noticed the unusual
layout of the road and a strange reoccurring rumbling.
Moving from the statue and further into the square, I realised
that cars were vanishing and reappearing in the blink of an
eye like apparitions, perhaps using the same gateway as the
Erl-King. And then I saw that Place Gutenberg was now
in fact the entrance to a large underground car park, used
for ease of access to the many luxury shops that lined the
surrounding streets. A sign near the opening of the labyrinth
stated *Parcus Gutenberg*. On previous trips, I would hear my
partner's parents refer to the car park simply as Gutenberg:
'Should we try Gutenberg for a space?' I moved back
towards the statue and sat at the foot of the plinth, watching
the cars reappear and disappear for some time, memories
vanishing and reappearing as the oncoming cold chilled the
bare skin of my legs. I was becoming curious about Brice's
words earlier and took the photograph of Monsieur Jacques
Cail out from the pages of Zola, looking deeply into its faded
tones. My eyes were constantly distracted by movements,
not just of cars but of other, more trying things; shadowy
shrouds seeming to dart around each corner. Even with
such ghosts, Place Gutenberg itself didn't seem quite real

anymore. History was more tangible than the present; it was a disconcerting thought. Perhaps because of the authentic paraphernalia I associated with Brice and his stall, the seller seemed more connected to the genuine nature of the place. More so than the actual city around me, the past was real, for that distant past had no presence of my father, alive or dead; a void away from his decision to wander to Crystal Palace Park and face one final public humiliation, as had been the general trend of his work when he was alive. Critics were his murderers, reviews his gallows.

The car park, the various shops and banks and restaurants all around seemed at odds with the statue. I considered Klotz's restoration projects for the cathedral, the man working at the same time as d'Angers on this statue; together, in their own ways, rejuvenating the public spaces of the city, then only decades away from being almost totally razed to the ground again by a variety of wars and conflicts. I only knew about Klotz from a tour I had taken around the cathedral some time previous, much to the dismay of my partner who wanted to wait in the American chain cafe around the corner. It was the only time I had been in the cathedral. I had laughed at Klotz's squat statue, the face looking shocked at still having to hold up the cathedral's pillars. It occurred then that information was *key*, that I could feel myself being absorbed *by* the city and moving away from any sense of having lost a father, just by recounting and learning about its history, scratching its streets onto my arms with my nails. I would rather consider Klotz crushed under stone or Gutenberg staring at lingerie, anything but the strange illusions in front of my eyes and the reality of England.

According to Brice, as he told me the following week, Madame Le Gall, a prominent socialite in the area, was often seen wearing her eccentric attire in Place Gutenberg, somewhat in keeping with the age of the buildings around; walking her dog and doing her utmost not to pay the least bit of attention to passers-by and their various stares at her unusual, extravagant clothing. I saw her several times in Place Gutenberg after that day and was told that she actually occupied a small apartment directly overlooking the statue of Gutenberg above the Aux Armes de Strasbourg restaurant where she often had heated arguments with the manager, Monsieur Cordeaux. I didn't know she was Madame Le Gall when I first spotted her as I sat on the step of Gutenberg's statue. She was almost as bizarre a sight as the Erl-King. Such arguments between Madame Le Gall and Monsieur Cordeaux concerned, so I was later told, the noise from merry drinkers who sat on the terrace of the restaurant at weekends in summer, and the various messes that Madame Le Gall's small dog left in exchange the following mornings by the entrance to the building's flats on Rue des Tonneliers. I was not to see Madame Le Gall for a while after the news regarding my father but her story, told in hindsight of seeing her surreal, floating image, was only one of dozens that somehow aided the etching of the streets upon my skin, upon my being. It occurred to me that, before meeting Brice again the following week, I should research Gutenberg further, if only to know whether or not he was being upfront with me.

I made my way back to my partner's flat in Petite France after an eternity of staring at bricks, ignoring the constant calls from my mother vibrating away in my bag, walking in long strides towards Grand'Rue, then veering left back towards the river and through Square des Moulins which my partner's apartment overlooked. The building I was staying in was a new construction, far more modern than the creaking buildings that could be seen from the windows. Square des Moulins and Ponts Couverts were much older and some of the chief tourist sites of the city due to their architecture. When in the lift of the building, I noticed that I had several more missed calls and messages from my mother, my harridan mother trying to *put this on me*, and so, with some trepidation, I rang to explain my half-formed plans for the coming weeks, even though they were still floating as her voice – clearly broken from a mixture of crying and satisfaction – cut through the dial tone. The conversation did not go well, though they never really had done and had always descended into raging battles. I sometimes lapsed into descriptions of Gutenberg's statue during our conversation and described what I had seen earlier that day, even mentioning briefly my conversation with Brice. Anything was preferable to addressing the questions she plied me with. How did the death make me *feel*? She would have loved to have known. When was I coming back to *sort everything out*? She wanted me to sort *everything*. How was I, the person supposedly most responsible now for my father, the failed painter, going to pay for all the costs of a death? She wanted me to pay for *everything*. Anything was better than considering such questions, so long as I did not have to face my father's body hanging from a tree in Crystal Palace Park. 'You must come back and sort out your father's *mess*,' she said. She was referring to his flat as much as the situation, a small ramshackle space, more canvas than

room, more paint than brick. I looked out absentmindedly
over Petite France and Square des Moulins, through the
flat's modern and incredibly vast windows, as it became
clear, even in my dazed state, that my mother, with each
frustrated sentence, was cutting off all ties with me. Not
that she had many; the Erl-King had more to say to me than
my own harridan mother. 'I must stay here and research
Strasbourg,' I said with a sense of disconnection that even
I found annoying and infuriating in hindsight. Anything I
could bluntly stab my mother with was of use. It was an airy
and pompous statement, but deliberate, as I knew it would
be easier to avoid everything to do with my father's death
by also avoiding my mother's acidic inquisition. 'But what
about the university and all of your work? You've spent the
last few months using it as an excuse to avoid everything
else and now, Isabelle, now, when I need you most, you're
chucking that out too,' she said, her voice trembling in
the way that had been so effective in years past in getting
money out of my ill father. Her voice was distorted by the
poor long-distance signal, as if Strasbourg was defending
me, as well as a seething anger which frosted the crackly
tones that managed to seep through the barriers. I could
feel her agitation growing at my lack of reaction to even her
most aggressive and insulting of suggestions. 'Coward. My
daughter is a coward. Spoilt, cowardly bitch; fucking spoilt,
cowardly bitch,' I heard her say, before she finally hung
up in the middle of my description of the panels adorning
Gutenberg's statue, the one with the writers. She hung up
as I was mid-sentence talking about Kant and his shocked,
pressurised skull; but I was glad, as her sonata of insults had
reached its natural cadence after a strenuous development

and recapitulation. She had always been like this. In a brief
moment of awareness, I connected Gutenberg's invention to
the variety of paperwork that would no doubt come my way
– or now, so I thought, come my mother's way. I imagined
wills, death certificates, funeral invoices, even perhaps a
note that my father may have left in a jacket pocket to be
found later upon his body, his old, brown corduroy perhaps.
That was his favourite jacket when painting. My mother,
aside from her detailed insinuations, had said very little.
I imagined that she would have hidden or destroyed any
such note anyway, especially if it expressed his reasons or
found final words of love or comfort for me. The guilt, for
there was guilt of course, subsided as I recalled the depiction
of the slaves being freed by Wilberforce. There were worse
things in this world than losing a father; there are worse
things in this world than losing a father; there will be worse
things in this world than losing a father.

I would not venture out of the flat for some days, sustaining
myself on the food left in the cupboards by my partner. I took
to researching Gutenberg's life and his achievements on a
dusty laptop. But, most importantly, I wanted to know about
his connections to Strasbourg. A message from my partner lit
up my phone, though the battery had been drained by my
mother. He had arrived safely in Argentina and would soon
be making his way around Buenos Aires before another trip
to somewhere further. His words didn't register particularly,
however, as I was scrolling through websites exploring
Gutenberg's life, providing a simple, almost mute answer of
clichéd affection to him in return. This had been our norm for
some time when separated in between our visits, almost like
being in love on automatic, which was arguably less love and

more habit. Though Gutenberg's innovations and moments
of ingenuity seem to have occurred when he lived and
worked in Strasbourg, he was born in Mainz in Germany, a
town just outside of Frankfurt which affectionately embraced
the bank of the River Rhine on the map, with more affection
than my own partner, in fact, who often felt like hugging a
stranger. There is scant detail regarding Gutenberg's early life
in general. Before his time in Strasbourg, I could find out very
little about him other than his family fled after an uprising
against the patricians and that a number of years in his life
appear mysteriously blank. A later letter confirmed him as
being back in Strasbourg, according to a paper written by a
man whose image thumbnail showed thick black glasses and
a nervous smile typically found in university academics with
little contact with the outside world. He was living not in the
square that would be later named after him, but in a church
further down the Ill tributary, near Quai du Brulig, called
Saint Arbogast, so named after the first Bishop of Strasbourg
who, in the seventh century and perhaps with some naivety,
brought Christianity to the province of Alsace. *You're a spoilt
bitch, Isabelle, didn't you hear?*

These so-called empty years of Gutenberg's life intrigued
me, as such a disappearing act seemed inconceivable
today with our constant monitoring and surveillance. In
all likelihood, these years were probably spent quietly in
between learning the trade of a goldsmith from his father
and gaining other skills. What most caught my attention,
however, was a little-discussed sideline of Gutenberg's that
was mentioned in an obscure online journal from a German
university. I even had to pay to access the journal, trading
the few euros via PayPal for a scrappy scan of a printed page

from an incredibly expensive volume which detailed the unusual sideline. It suggested that Gutenberg, while learning the craft of jewel cutting and the general skills required of a jeweller, sparked a business idea with one of his students, Andreas Dritzehn, along with several other colleagues. The scheme was this: to make and manufacture a number of 'holy mirrors' made from polished glass. It was one of the skills that Gutenberg had become exemplary in and had since taught to several eager students. Such mirrors, so the plan went, were to be sold to pilgrims on their wanderings towards a very particular set of holy relics. The mirrors were not designed to give luck on their pilgrimage or to help when needing to fix their attire, but instead for something unusually practical in nature – unusual considering its esoteric potential at least. It was suggested that such mirrors could capture and somehow contain whatever power was emanating from a holy relic. Rather like a flask taken to a well or spring to gather fresh water, the holy mirror could then be covered with a thin cloth, ergo trapping the powerful rays derived from the transcendent and put to use whenever needed; perhaps when an ill loved one was in distress, or when a business was failing. I longed for a holy mirror filled with the divine, perhaps to shine upon the Erl-King when he dared show himself in full. Gutenberg's plan seemed auspicious, with the pilgrims targeted on their route to Aachen on the border between Germany and Belgium where, every seven years since 1238, a number of the relics owned by and contained in the town's cathedral were displayed to the public in order for their holy aura to be shared and made use of. In Gutenberg's eyes, this was the well from which his lucrative flasks would be filled.

These four relics, held by the cathedral since the time of Charlemagne, were said to be comprised of Mary's robe worn on the night on which Jesus was born; the swaddling clothes Mary used to protect the baby; Jesus' loincloth, said to be his last covering before his death on the cross, which to my mind felt a little fetishistic; and another cloth used to wrap and cover the decapitated head of John the Baptist. Gutenberg, Dritzehn and his partners made preparations for the mirrors, so the article suggested, spending a great deal of time experimenting with differing techniques of glass polishing before finalising a batch that was ready for sale. The project, however, was to fail, at least that year, rather like my father's paintings had seemed to constantly fail. For, with the effort made in planning and producing the items, they had miscalculated the date when the Aachen pilgrims would be in the vicinity of Strasbourg, now changed due to a flood, and the pilgrimage moved to the following year. Much to their dismay, they lost their money through this miscalculation. When reading about this in the journal, I could not help but smile. I imagined, albeit melodramatically, the four men in question carrying their wares, rather like Brice and his fellow trinket sellers, to some empty country road on the outskirts of the city and waiting until several dark nights had descended and passed before realising that no one was coming. Gutenberg could, of course, have waited another year, perhaps considering the mirrors as a nest egg of sorts, ready to make a great deal of money from the next pilgrimage, though they did eventually manage to regain their investment money sometime later.

Gutenberg, however, like most desperate entrepreneurs, was not to be put off by this in spite of a growing trail of legal disputes, lawsuits and debts following behind him like a spectre of failure. He continued working with Dritzehn and the other two men, Hans Riffe and Andreas Heilmann, drawing all three into a contract for his latest, as yet secret, project. *Your father is dead, Isabelle.* Why the men agreed is not quite certain, especially considering Gutenberg's many sporadic failures and his increasing need for investment in a project secretively named *aventur und kunst*. All was not to go as planned at first with Gutenberg's chief partner dying of plague, never to see his tutor flourish with his groundbreaking invention. The contract they had signed meant that Dritzehn's brother then insisted on access to all information and rights regarding the secret project. Like many of the markers in Gutenberg's life, it was a legal ramification that was to prove immovable, the interloper winning rights to anything that Gutenberg produced via his new machine. There was, at least in what I could find on websites, internet databases and journal libraries online, no record of any progress – and by progress, I mean the production of any official printed work – when Gutenberg was still in the city but, in all probability and due to the legal clause meaning he would lose some part of anything now produced by his process, he most likely did and simply kept it a secret; like the ray from a holy relic trapped and contained within the mirror walls of his mind.

Gutenberg's innovation was not simply in the printing press but in the ability to move it around. He travelled back to Mainz in search of funding, securing it and setting up a workshop where printing began with several small textbooks on Latin. My father used to pretend he could read Latin, though when a friend from my previous department in Brighton had visited, this lie had been exposed. We had always had to face such disappointing realities with him as the years went on. I began to lose interest in Gutenberg's life at this point, mostly because the journals seemed to continually repeat the same aspects. Recognition seemed to have only come to him mere years before he died, exiled in Eltville to the north-west of Mainz. The only other two aspects that really sparked my interest were to do with his body, not least because it was, obviously, not hung from a tree in Crystal Palace Park. That he was buried in a graveyard that was subsequently destroyed, rendering his grave now lost and unknown, seemed ironic for the man who provided the technology with which to communicate, share and save for posterity the most thoughtless and worthless of ideas. But the journal suggested something I found more disturbing: that no image of the man was derived from any genuine likeness, the first depiction of him being made almost exactly a hundred years after his death. It was then that I realised that I could not, mere hours after hearing of his death, remember what my father's face looked like. Who was, therefore, the man that overlooked Place Gutenberg, holding the famous Bibles? Who was the man hanging from the tree in Crystal Palace Park? They could be one and the same. A sense of disappearance came over me and, in the following days of idly researching for minor facts and notes about Gutenberg himself, I felt envious of such a feat.

The man that stood over the square, the man fashioned and recreated by Pierre-Jean David d'Angers, could have been anyone. Days passed slowly with only slight pauses from daydreams, moments marked by spotting shadowy movements on the streets below at night, a feeling of hands sometimes caressing my naked back during twilight hours and words provided by messages from my partner detailing his equally slow journey across South America. It was a pleasant distraction from the feeling of something solid permanently climbing my throat as if I was about to cry and shout, determined not to turn around whenever I felt something brush against my shoulders or the touch of the Erl-King, which I did my best to deny my fearful excitement over. In a message, I told my partner briefly about my research and my plan to stay in his flat, highlighting most importantly that I would pay the bills, though the messages obviously failed in inducing any interest, especially in contrast to the excitement he was probably having. As long as I paid my way, he wouldn't care, I thought. I missed the feel of his thighs behind mine and the way his hair sprang back under my hands when ruffled, but that was all. And these things were interchangeable with anyone. I would sit looking out of the window towards the cathedral which loomed over the buildings in front of his desk, a view I was always envious of when back in London. My office view was a brick wall, my flat's view another's window in which bodies, clothed and naked, would casually pass by like footage from old silent films.

It occurred to me that the imposter posing as Gutenberg was standing guard over the car park almost directly ahead of me behind the rows of lower buildings; looking on even if I could not see him. Before the day I had arranged to meet Brice arrived, my interest in Gutenberg and Strasbourg moved on finally to the phrase he labelled his printing project: *aventur und kunst*. Adventure and Art. The art aspect I could understand instantly: the fame of the printing's beauty, the detail, and Gutenberg's desire to make a work of art that would sit alongside the ornate written word rather than merely replace it – all were easy to grasp. There was a reason why his work fetched the great sums of money at extravagant auctions in New York, Paris and London, more often reserved for the names of noted artists. But it was the 'adventure' part that I pondered over. I could not help but project my own sense of dislocation onto the phrase, assuming adventure at first to be some form of physical travel. But it seemed to miss the point, as Gutenberg, with the little that the journal could tell me, only appears to have moved when exiled, forced out, or in swift haste to avoid the legal fallout of some lawsuit. I pictured the man's face as blank, rather than as the bearded intellectual who would have preferred the stability of a home; a man who would have preferred to stay in Strasbourg and define his printing technique without the trouble of being sued. Was the adventure an intellectual one? The literal meaning was 'enterprise', clearly a reference to business more than anything else, the cold reality of finance. I felt the streets carve themselves upon my arms more and more as the information was gathered, the pain causing sharp but pleasurable intakes of breath, and I made little jottings on bright pink Post-it notes when the canvas of my body had had enough; as if the more I learnt, the less of a person I became. I was becoming a map of the city's history, slowly engraved and measured out via flesh and blood. As if being wrung and crushed through one of Gutenberg's printing presses, Strasbourg was slowly making its mark upon me, its imprint gradually defined; a perfect art of avoidance. My father's feet hadn't appeared at the corner of my eye during those later days of research, only the swift shroud sometimes daring to show itself by the corner of a building over the road or over the bridge, and so I concluded that my plan was working. The mirror captures, even reflections of fiends. What had been a spur-of-the-moment idea and a chance conversation when reeling from the news of a death, delivered in the most deliberately blunt and uncaring fashion by my spiteful mother, was proving worthwhile. There was no real mystery here. The night before the day of the fair on Rue du Vieux-Marché-aux-Poissons descended, the clouds were hanging low in the sky, obscuring the tip of the cathedral which was lit with a strangely yellow aura. It looked, more than anything else, like a projection upon the sky or, as I thought more aptly, an *imprint* of a building, stamped there by some fantastical contraption. My meeting with Brice was due the following morning and I wondered what yarn of enterprise and art he would spin over the morning's passing.

It is thought by many that the Keller Group – a mixture of explorers, botanists, geologists and artists, all from the city of Strasbourg – was one of the key instigators of the *Naturkunst* revival of the last century. The group produced visual art and writing with a basis of creative endeavour in the rigour of natural history and science, but in a more casual and empathetic way than such individual fields often required. The movement, of which the Keller Group – whose name still remains a mystery – was only one of a number of similar landscape-based movements from its era, desired a breakdown in the barriers between the arts and the sciences, foreshadowing the growth of many divides that still figure today in academia, culture and universities. It is ironic that the divide was arguably smaller at the time of their work than it would be some 120 years later. Jean Felder was its key figure, a writer and poet interested in the writing of Goethe and the scientific tracts of Louis Ramond, a noted botanist of Strasbourg, both of whom Felder shared some history with having studied at the University of Strasbourg as they had done and having also possessed a desire to write in the German Romantic tradition. Felder, however, is considered someone still stuck in the Symbolist tradition rather than the coming Modernism of his time; nature dragging back the obscurity of the previous movement's allusions, since indecipherable. Unlike Ramond, however, Felder stuck with his desire to write winding prose poems and balanced this with an interest in certain forms of plant life; an interest he explored regularly by accompanying various scientific expeditions out of Strasbourg, sometimes to the mountainous area around northern Switzerland and Basel, sometimes venturing further north to the mountains that sit around the outer reaches of the Bas-Rhin and towards the Haut-Rhin.

Felder took to accompanying the members of a botanical clique formed in the department at the university led by Max Leiber and Anton François, the latter said to be an actual descendant of Ramond himself, several relatives down the line, though this has never been substantiated and can be considered an ambitious gambit at best. Anton François helped define the movement of modern *Naturkunst* as he was also a keen painter, basing his practice around watercolour images of plant specimens but soon moving into more academic and theoretical work in the days when other creative movements were founding their violently industrial interventions. Allowing a number of other noted figures from the Bas-Rhin arts circles into the group, including Eleanor François – Anton's wife and a noted phytological artist in her own right – and early collage specialist Fabrice Perrin (foreshadowing the methods used by Georges Braque), the group ventured on many expeditions looking for inspiration, both for their phytological research and what could be described as a French equivalent to the spiritual qualities found in the writing of the American Transcendentalists. Like Ralph Waldo Emerson and Henry David Thoreau, Felder and the others desired a more spiritual end to their walks and explorations, not least because Felder himself was in deep but quiet mourning for his parents, said, when he was younger, to have gone through with a suicide pact in the period of Strasbourg's history when the town was annexed by the burgeoning German Empire. The Keller Group became somewhat associated with certain free utopian movements who equally sought refuge from Europe's political strife in many rural climes and with a particular emphasis on the forests. Felder, whose body of work was largely destroyed

in a fire at a private gallery in the 1970s, long after he had
purportedly died, became so enamoured with the idea of
living outside of any defined notion of urban system that
he was said to be more regularly living outside than inside.
The botanical elements of the Keller Group were reputed
to have taken to leaving him in the forests below the ridge
of the mountain range that traversed the two departments
of Alsace towards the end of their main period of activity.
Many photos exist of the group, now housed in the city's
museum on Rue du Vieux-Marché-aux-Poissons, along with
a handful of surviving works of Felder's from the gallery
fire, though even these are largely ashen and charred. Being
a strict vegetarian, it is unlikely that Felder would have been
happy with this outcome considering that the building that
the museum is now housed in was one of the city's first
abattoirs. In their more hopeful days, however, the Keller
Group would document every trip and would travel no
matter what the weather into the countryside in search
of new knowledge regarding plants and specimens, with
particular focus on various adaptations to the environment.
In one photograph, preserved and on permanent display in
a private Strasbourg museum, the three main participants
of the group, along with an unnamed fourth, can be seen
journeying upon a stony outcrop in a forest clearly in the
straits of winter.

Felder can be seen on the far right, his body clearly less adorned with equipment than the botanists Leiber (left) and François (centre). In some ways, Anton François' likeness to the portraits that survive of Louis Ramond can be partly distinguished in his heavy brow and deep-set eyes, though the likeness was said to be more uncanny when seen in the flesh. It was natural that the man, in his field, played upon such a likeness to improve his social standing. In François' diary, housed in the University of Strasbourg's archive, his delight at the group's work and research is clearly perceptible. 'The work,' so he wrote, 'fills me with a great and profound joy; to know that ideas can take so many routes, not least those of the journal, the paper or the lecture, but things, as in Jean's wonderful work, that must surely in all of their wondrous delight, fill even the most uneducated of Strasbourg, no, *Frenchman*, in fact – I can write as I please! – fill the most uneducated *Frenchman* with the delight of God's creation and His world.' The journal is filled with such passages, marking a pleasant period in the group's work, even with the calamitous politics raging over the continent at their time of exploration. Though the group, and François in particular, are noted for their pride at incorporating Felder's work and that of the other artists into their scientific esteem, the same confidence was not ultimately shared by Felder in particular who, besides questioning the quality of the creative work put alongside his by several of the scientists (especially Leiber's poetry which is, by any account, considered atrocious pastoral nonsense), was deeply uncertain about the qualities of his own work, especially his painting, which he would often leave in the forests for weeks at a time in the hope that the environment would somehow improve them. Towards the end of the group's relations, strained by the political situation in Strasbourg and the impending wars of the twentieth century, Felder took to setting off alone into the woods, sometimes to check on left canvases, sometimes to – in the words of an early, surviving interview with *Journal des Beaux-Arts* printed many years later – 'lose himself amongst the trees'. It was during one of these visits out of the city, leaving his small flat in Rue du Jeu-des-Enfants, that the artist disappeared and a search was organised by the remaining members of the group once he was missed, in spite of the growing rift between them. Several had already left the area to avoid various conflicts brewing on the border, however. A photograph was handed out to each member of the search party, one of which survives. The cross drawn on, most probably by Anton François, resides above the head of Jean Felder.

Such efforts went unrewarded and, after several weeks of searching, sometimes as a group, sometimes individually, Felder was pronounced missing presumed dead. His body was never found and his work passed into private hands, eventually to suffer the fate of the flames, though local folklore in creative circles dramatises the fire as being somehow caused by Felder himself, now impossibly old, surviving but angry at the commercialisation of his creative endeavours and wreaking a terrible revenge on the art market. Anton François himself would die a little later in the Great War, though it is uncertain what happened to Max Leiber as most records regarding many of the group were lost in the conflict, which destroyed great portions of various

buildings and archives. Many years later, in the 1950s, some
clothes and work presumed to be Felder's were found by a
group of young hikers, though the likelihood of them being
his was deemed so acutely remote that they were sold to a
local junk shop and lost again, such a find only marked by a
local newspaper story. Of Felder's work, many art historians
contest whether he had any influence at all, though some
suggest this to be in line with the overly harsh character of
art criticism after both world wars. One prominent critic
and scholar linked with the Frankfurt School suggested, in
a typically cruel streak of analysis, that Felder, the 'naïve
optimist as to the quality and power of his own work', was
probably right to walk off into the woods, if only to avoid
the crash of society's brutal wave upon his 'delicate mental
shoreline'. This was itself attacked by several later critics,
the most prominent of which, Edvard Seelig, suggested that
only someone of the Frankfurt School could have failed to
see the quality of the 'supernatural light' that eventually
found its way into Felder's surviving work; such was its
power that, like certain folkloric curios from the early years
of the Enlightenment, it seemingly had the ability to contain
the natural essence absorbed from its surroundings – the
artist briefly allowing access to pure divinity as if days had
been spent in witness to a majestic, transcendental visitation.

The sky was moon-grey on the morning I was to meet Brice.
I had woken up from another sleepless night in the flat,
the many street lights around Petite France illuminating
the bedroom with a variety of white and red hues. There

were no curtains, something I had often commented on to my partner who suggested curtains weren't necessary. His bemusement at net curtains on visiting London had always been palpable. The only option for subduing such light in the flat was by lowering heavy wooden shutters constructed from dark, thin slats housed on the outside of the building, and levered down from the inside by a steel chain. It left a choice between a total, engulfing darkness or a spattered grey with flashes and shadows perceptible even with eyes closed, so the latter was always to be the better option. Darkness had taken on an unusual atmosphere since hearing of my father's death. It was too much of a blank canvas upon which anything could be dreamt up to play and dance upon. Trying for two nights to sleep with the shutters down led to my being transported to a wet forest; the sound of water dripping loudly from the leaves and branches of trees that resided there. In the forest, I was running from something, the sound of branches cracking, not from footfall but higher up, as if something flew out of the void after me, hovering several feet in the air but towards me all the same. I could make out the view, lying on my back in bed but staring out through the creaking woodland that extended as a vision through the darkness of the ceiling, even making out shapes constructed, quite by accident, through the certain crossings of twigs and bark. At almost any point, however, this woodland could turn quickly into a trap, for, surrounded by trees, I would find myself stuck in the company of my father's body or worse. The blackness of the room would always allow only a glimpse of him hanging deathly still, not even swaying in the breeze, before whatever was following caught up. But a glimpse would be enough before

I would find my body rattled with fear, jolting breathlessly
forward to discover the bedside table on which stood a small
lamp. The light would fill the room in a snap, exorcising the
haunted forest and my father's body to faraway realms,
back to the boundaries of Crystal Palace Park which were
thankfully in the distance on the sinking isle.

On my desk was an assortment of items: printouts of
the scans of pages from the journal entry about Gutenberg,
with several sentences and names underlined in red biro;
a box of low-quality cough sweets with a strange chemical
flavour that I had taken to eating copiously; a half-drunk
glass of water; a small pile of books I had brought to
Strasbourg to read and which, aside from the volume of
Zola, had since been finished; a cuddly toy of a monkey
character from a cartoon film that my partner had insisted
on placing next to the bed for good luck; and a notepad
upon which I had made brief jottings for a short paper I
was ultimately never to write. This table had never really
changed during my stay, with the exception of which book
took precedence on the pile. Even my awakenings with the
shutters up were forcibly early, sleep stolen away by various
worries and the merest hint of sunlight. The desk would be
a comforting presence and, when unable to sleep, I would
sit at it for hours among the mess of my partner's medical
books, staring at the cathedral's silhouette cast upon the
skyline. I wondered on that particular morning what time
Brice would be up and, from the experience of having had
a table at a car boot sale during childhood at my mother's
insistence, assumed he would also be awake, prepping his
items into an arranged order in his car, going through some
morning routine that was far healthier and fuller than my

own, and unpacking his goods onto the pasting tables set up on Rue du Vieux-Marché-aux-Poissons. It gave me a strange pleasure to consider that, in spite of the phosphorous darkness still hanging over Strasbourg, we were both, in all probability, awake and experiencing it. I stood at the large windows for some time, looking down onto the few short bursts of life that flittered around the Ponts Couverts. An old beggar woman, who always wore red and would regularly ask for change, was hunched over and walking with her usual staggered gait along the path of the bridge, carefully avoiding its cobbles. A man was delivering what looked to be bread behind the back of the Marco Polo restaurant that lay directly on the bank of the river. Another man, riding a moped, was speeding onto the Ponts Couverts without due caution and quickly swerved right into what is now a car park. There was no shroud, thankfully; whatever was in the forest of my dreams could not show itself then. I felt worried as the first sun's rays began to stream gently through the sky. It looked as if it could rain, the clouds hanging heavy, and I could certainly not see Brice setting up his table if there was rainfall due. Some of the stalls, including a stall I had once bought an old cigarette case from with the initials 'J.F.' engraved upon it, had tent-like covers for such situations. But Brice did not have one of these tents when I first met him, and I assumed – correctly, as I later found out – that he did not possess one. 'It's all or nothing with this fair, and the slightest problem… well, you may as well go home,' he said later that day. The rain had held off and, though not a warm or sunny day, it was an amiable enough autumn morning for a fair of trinkets. It occurred to me, having been awake for several hours and about to leave the flat, that I had been waiting all week for this day; perhaps even this moment, when there was once more a necessity and purpose in having to go outside. I had carved the history of the city onto my body and mind but had done very little walking or exploring since last seeing Brice at the fair. I was haunting the city as a ghost, treacling its past via a computer screen.

Leaving the flat, I breathed the air afresh once more and took in the noise of other people with pleasure. Passers-by were talking loudly and quickly; I could only hear fragments of their speech which, due to their typical animation in talking, seemed impossibly important. An ambulance went by with the siren whirring, the hospital and its various buildings being directly behind Rue du Cygne. There was the cry of a moorhen that was using a box in the water nearby as a nest, sometimes defending its territory from a pair of great crested grebes that I had pointed out excitedly to my partner in the summer, receiving only a shrug of the shoulders in return. He seemed to have an aversion to things I found interesting, an aspect of his personality I only realised in hindsight during his prolonged absences, but handily forgot in his presence when the sheer physical pleasure of being reunited swamped everything for a time. I followed the river, after meandering around Petite France, which seemed like a moat protecting the very heart of Strasbourg from calamity, all of the way to Pont du Corbeau where the bridge leading to Rue du Vieux-Marché-aux-Poissons crossed the water. Though other bridges crossed the water, none were as evocative as this one, I thought. The bridge had historical relevance, with a stone monument referring to its gruesome past along with a plastic tourist board detailing its history. The bridge, so the board said, was actually named locally as the Bridge of Tortures or Butcher's Bridge – *Schindbrücke* – and was where many of the city's public executions were carried out. Bodies were kept in cages, often still living, so that the public passing over the bridge could see and perhaps taunt those held there. *Your father was trapped, Isabelle – you were his cage, our cage.* Men were usually drowned, though some died from their treatment and their corpses were simply lowered into the water. *Corbeau* – raven – probably refers to the bird's prevalence in such areas of death, feeding on the eyes of men; blinded before their time. I was happy to find a postcard of the bridge several weeks later in the shop of antiquity over the way from my partner's flat, developing my little collection of curios as the weeks went by.

The fair's stalls could be seen instantly on both sides of the bridge and so, wishing to savour the day and not rush straight into Brice's story, I took to browsing the tables once more. Each stall was a cacophony of objects, all shouting for their story to be heard, to be taken out of the flowing, meaningless white noise of history and to be given purpose and voice. There were old glass beer bottles, perhaps clinked together in pleasure when first full; boxes of postcards sent by the dead to the dead with thoughts and kindness; piles of battered watches, all the more deceased due to their lack of ticking but which perhaps had once been essential in meeting loved ones in those early first days of courting; and an array of small paintings and furniture that felt conspicuous when not housed in some homely setting. As always, I felt sorry for these objects, and took to handling several in the hope of passing on some warmth, some feeling that they were not still forgotten. I acknowledged them through this handling and touching, just for a brief moment. I crossed the bridge

and began to search for Brice's stall. There seemed to be
more tables than usual, and certainly more than the previous
week, so it took more time to find the old man. Eventually,
I came to the final row of stalls that lined Place des Tripiers
and spotted his table not far from where it was the previous
week. I noticed it, not by seeing him, for he was as good as
hidden when sat hunched over on the fold-up chair behind
his items, but by a cut-glass vase that he had filled with what
looked to be smoothed pebbles from a beach. I remembered
noticing it during my first conversation with him, though I
was too drawn into the mystery of Monsieur Jacques Cail
and his photograph to pay it more attention. I could feel
the photograph's edges rubbing against my fingers as it
stuck out of the thin, mostly empty purse jammed into my
coat pocket. I had thought it best to bring it along in case
it somehow completed or aided Brice's story. I pretended
to browse at a neighbouring table while he sold an old
wooden cup to an ancient-looking woman before he spotted
me and cried a surprisingly delighted welcome, clapping
his hands and reaching out over the table to greet me. I
wandered over and shook his outstretched hand before
Brice indicated a second, slightly damp looking fold-up
chair leaning against a box, which I opened and positioned
next to him. '*Ça va?*' he asked, and we spoke briefly in
French before he accommodated me and switched to his
excellent English. Our small talk barely lasted before he
began to move the conversation on to what had drawn us
back together. 'Have you got the photograph of Jacques?'
he asked, and I brought it out, along with a folded receipt
from the supermarket which had accidently attached itself
to the photo with a loving embrace. He looked at it before

putting it down in a gap on the table in front of us, pulling two more photographs from his pocket which he then laid on top. 'It took me a while to find these,' he said. 'I haven't thought about this for a long time, strange considering how close I am to Gutenberg's monument every week!' He reached behind the chair and pulled up a flask and some plastic cups with awkward square handles, offering and then pouring two mugs of green tea. The heat of the drink meeting autumn's oncoming cold created great spectres of steam in front of us, though I was grateful for the warmth it provided my hands as I sat cradling it, feeling distinctly more human than I had done in previous days. 'I'm glad you came back. Finding the photos meant finding the memories and it would have been such a waste if I couldn't tell it to someone once I'd dug them out,' he said. I sat back in the chair, ready to listen to Brice unfold his tale, still vaguely suspicious of him trying to sell me some trinket, supposedly of great worth; that all of this was some elaborate patter in which to part company with some piece of rubbish. 'I was uncertain whether to sell that photo initially, but I just didn't feel I needed it anymore,' he mumbled. 'It was part of a set of three which I know the history of incredibly well, though I never met Jacques himself, only heard about him.' He interspersed his story with methodical sips of his green tea from the yellow cup and occasional pauses to acknowledge customers momentarily eyeing up the old pens, faded soft toys, framed Pierre-Auguste Renoir prints and the rest of his paraphernalia for sale. 'That photo was one of two that I have of Jacques, the other is this one.' He pulled the first photograph from the pile on the table and handed it to me.

I noticed Cail instantly, with his seemingly never-ending cheek and the feeling that his ear was only momentarily remembered during the final moments of his creation. The look on his face was incredibly similar to the photo I had bought but the change in his clothes was stark. He was now in an army uniform rather than the extravagant suit, hat and cane that he had in the garden in 1902. The collar made him look far tidier and less dandyish than the clothing worn in the other photo. The photo was a family portrait, his wife on the left, with dark eyes and neat hair, clearly struggling to hide her unhappiness; unhappiness at her husband leaving for war, perhaps. People often looked unhappy in older photos, as if the process of having it taken was still something suspicious, something to be cautious of. My partner often felt the same, though only because he was decidedly paranoid about his side profile, from which the shape of his nose was undeniably more prominent. The son in the centre of Brice's old photograph also seemed unusual, his haircut so severe as to seem almost false and stuck upon his head with glue, an effect caused by the large forehead which he clearly inherited from his father. I wagered when first considering the photo that the photographer had asked the boy to try and look angelic, the pose seeming an attempt to emulate an innocent cherub but coming across as merely unusual and forced. 'Cail's wife, Marianne, was increasingly unhappy with him for joining just on the brink of war,' Brice said. 'They had lived happily in a house in a small town on the outskirts of Strasbourg. Marianne would stay at home to look after their son, Charles, while Jacques was, like myself, a trader in curios and antiques. That's partly why I was interested in him.' I let the seller continue his story but could not help staring dreamily into the pictures, feeling the world around me dissolve and reassert itself in a previous time. Sometimes my phone would vibrate in my pocket, bringing me out of these past visions, but that was all. Emails could wait, as I had little intention of answering any of them.

Brice told of Jacques' small shop that he had on Rue du Ciel; a place where I once bumped into and almost knocked over an old man who I showered quickly with profuse apologies in both French and English, to little effect. 'The shop that Jacques owned was said to specialise in smaller curios. He would have liked the fair we have here now,' Brice added. 'There was supposedly no furniture or larger items of any sort in his shop but lots of curios such as snuff boxes, cigarette cards, jewellery, Chinese puzzle boxes, silver wear, that sort of thing. Now,' Brice said, 'here is the interesting thing. I know for a fact that Jacques was, for a time, unusually obsessed with Johannes Gutenberg. Ahh, I know what you're thinking. You think I'm going to pull out a Bible? Sadly no, that was not Jacques' interest, though I'm sure he wouldn't have turned down the offer of one, of course!' I wondered where the conversation was going, sipping my tea once more but now finding it too cold to drink. The seller asked how much I knew about Gutenberg and I could not help but lie. 'Oh, not much, I didn't even know that statue of him was there until we met last week,' I said. This was perfectly true, though I felt my mouth running as I spoke of the fact that we had no real likeness for Gutenberg himself and that the statue, as interesting and formidable as it was, could effectively have been of anyone. The man who revolutionised the sharing of information was forever a facsimile, a guess. *Don't forget your father's birthday, you're always heartless and forget the important things; spiteful daughter.* It was the sort of information that almost gave away my days of obsessive research regarding the man. Brice, however, did not suspect a thing and so he continued on with his story. 'Well,' he said, 'Cail was obsessed with Gutenberg, not because of the possibility of finding a printed work but something else. He had got wind of someone in possession of a valuable object connected to the man. Gutenberg was a goldsmith among other things, and before he went into printing he made mirrors, you know. They were no ordinary mirrors, however, but mirrors sold to pilgrims travelling through the city. Someone in Strasbourg, Cail learned, had one of these mirrors, and I know that he was obsessed with finding it. It strained his marriage with Marianne, poor woman. The man supposedly called upon every house in the centre of Strasbourg in search of the owner of this mirror until everyone thought him mad. I think, if I remember the story correctly, that the obsession developed into a belief in the mirror's powers or some such rubbish, using that as the excuse for spending days and nights away from his wife and young child.' Brice paused and I began to take in the story.

I knew exactly which mirrors he spoke of, though the importance that the man had placed upon them seemed surreal. The journal article had, rightly or wrongly, portrayed it as an almost scandalous hoax, at most an attempt to obtain money quickly, probably to pay the debts that Gutenberg owed from previous lawsuits. I could see the mirror in my mind's eye, perhaps contained in an ornate wooden box for dramatic presentation. I could see the scratches which had opened out into small circles of rust and an incredibly tattered piece of fabric hanging over its glass, once purple but now faded to a light brown. I felt and shared in Jacques' obsession, considering the power of the item and what it could have meant. For someone from so recent a period in history, centuries after the Enlightenment that Gutenberg foreshadowed, to believe that the mirror could contain some powerful, otherworldly essence, rendered the photos of the man in a different light. He still did not seem obsessive, no matter how long I looked searchingly into his face. But the potential for *something* was there. It was an open, family face. Something I knew only because it seemed in every way opposite to my father's and my mother's. 'He found it, you know,' Brice cut in suddenly, bringing me out of my daydream. 'He found it and its owner, buying it for an incredibly low price from an old man who lived near the cathedral. It was only a year or two before the war and he had spent all that precious time before it searching for one thing only. And then he found it and his life, I assume, seemed empty, perhaps even wasted. That's when he decided to fight, not that there was much choice of course. Perhaps he felt drained or was disappointed by the mirror. No one ever saw it and he hid it before he left, but I don't know where. Perhaps he destroyed it or threw it into the river, who knows. Whenever I think about it, I sometimes see a bright spot in the river, you know, the light hitting it in a strange way as if the mirror was lodged in the mud somewhere near Petite France. But it's never there; it's just the sun playing tricks. It's probably lost forever.' He picked up the third picture, looking at it with a sense of sadness which shone only for a second before handing it to me. The picture was of another man, many years hence from the previous pictures judging by the fashion. It was incredibly atmospheric, so I thought, the man standing alone in a thin avenue of trees, turned foggy by the aging process of the print. Even more unusual was the man's posture. The way he was standing seemed unusual. I felt I had seen his face somewhere before. It looked as if his right hip sunk lower than usual whenever he leaned upon it, further emphasised by the man's jacket, which hid the hip line and made his torso seem ill-fitting with his legs. The sight of the trees with their thick bark irked me slightly too, reminding me of the trees which I assumed my father had found sturdy enough to take the strain, or of forests where dark creatures searched for broken teeth and the souls of infants.

'This is Charles grown-up,' Brice said as he poured himself another cup of green tea. Of course it was, I thought. I could see it in his face instantly: the strange, half-shocked, half-amused expression seen in his failed attempt at cherub-like charm in the other photo. Charles Cail, all grown-up without a father. We were uncomfortably similar in some ways. 'Jacques was killed pretty early on in the war,' Brice continued, 'and Marianne Cail was driven to despair with the news. Charles grew up quickly and, by the end of the war, was taking care of her even though he was still young. His father's business had been closed but not sold or taken over and so, when finally old enough to look for work, he sought to carry on in Jacques' footsteps. This was much later, after the war. Charles couldn't fight, of course, being still a child. France was tired and certainly not in the business of collecting trinkets anymore,' he said. 'But I know that Charles persisted, eventually making the business work even if it cost him a great deal of his own health. He married, had a child and, again like his father, developed an interest in the Gutenberg mirror even with another war brewing; how he survived that I don't know. The thing was a curse, really. He had found his father's notes apparently and, right up until his own death in the early, err... eighties – yes, that's how it is said – was equally passionate about finding the lost mirror. He didn't find it, naturally, and died totally miserable in a retirement home near Truchtersheim. *Aventur und kunst, mon ami,'* he said with a smile. *'Aventur und kunst. C'est tout.'*

I wasn't sure what to make of Brice's story, and sat in consideration for a while as we both watched the passers-by inspect and explore the items on the table, though never bothering to buy anything. After minor conversations about some of his regular customers and local characters, a silence grew between us as it became clear neither of us knew what else to say or why, in that week, we had both felt the need to be joined by this story; why Brice needed to tell it and why I, never having met the man or having heard of Gutenberg's mirror until that very week, felt the need to listen. Yet I knew, even while in the depths of this experience, that I needed more like it, more such distractions from Erl-Kings in the shadows. I felt my body, deflated by a silent mourning which I had done my best to ignore, now alive and with new vigour. I was grateful to Brice for telling this story, though after some further moments of silence he broke it by expressing his apologies that he wouldn't be able to sell me the other two photos, placing them in his own wallet quickly after letting me take photos of them on my phone. 'Oh, that's fine,' I said, getting up to excuse myself and say farewell, feeling the damp backs of my legs from having sat on the fold-up chair. It was unusual feeling my body in that moment, having forgotten properly what touch felt like, unconsciously enjoying the caress of my own hands before I became aware of how strange it would have seemed to continue. I was desperate for human warmth or even some cold, erotic release that would be forgotten within hours. But equally I felt only capable of minor communication, unable to fulfil any objective but my own physical presence, even that fading into vagueness. I had expected Brice to reveal the mirror from within some bag and attempt to barter for its sale. But he simply sat there mournfully. 'And who was Charles?' I finally asked Brice before making to leave. It had been a long morning, and I expected the merchant would be grateful for the space to try and make a few euros before the day slid away into the veil of the night. 'Oh Charles,' he mumbled, looking in the direction of Place Gutenberg once more, avoiding my gaze. 'He was my father.'

It was Saint Valentine's Day in 1347 when Strasbourg first enacted a fully fledged anti-Semitic policy. While maintaining its own authority in the region, the city was struck by a great plague which claimed the lives of many of its citizens. Unsure as to the plague's cause, many of the city's authorities soon lay the blame for the subsequent deaths at the feet of the city's Jewish population, which was minimal but not wholly invisible. Such was their fear of this minority group that several believed them to be secretly in league, concocting and plotting a takeover of the city via the poisoning of the many wells which were vital for the supply of clean water. It was on this day that, after a brewing suspicion founded on little else but despair at the cause of a great and sweeping malady, the Jews were violently expelled from the city, many of them killed in the process, eventually culminating in an extensive massacre two years later in 1349. After this, and in spite of the plague dying down, the remaining Jews were only allowed within the city walls during daytime in order to barter their particular trades to the townsfolk, and were forced outside the gates of the city after ten o'clock at night. The policy was to last for several hundred years before the community finally found a representative in the form of Cerf Beer of Medelsheim, a respected and successful man who had a house in what is now the Finkwiller quarter near Petite France. Thanks to being on good terms with King Louis XV, Cerf Beer evaded the Jewish ruling imposed in Strasbourg and campaigned against various anti-Semitic crimes still occurring in the region. He fought against such a policy, arranging for the gradual return of the citizens to the area he lived, actually more traditionally famed for being the place of residence of many of the city's gardeners. He eventually died during the Reign of Terror after being released from a year in prison for suspected royal allegiances. The site of his house is now symbolised by a memorial plaque adjacent to the school on Quai Charles Frey, just in front of the Hôtel du Dragon.

Much of this was researched heavily many years hence by a noted academic teaching at the University of Strasbourg's ethnography department: the writer and polemicist, Gabriel David. Being purportedly half-Jewish on his mother's side in the period leading up to the Second World War, David was a prominent historian of the Jewish history of the Bas-Rhin and Haut-Rhin. His flamboyant nature was often called attention to by many locals, especially in regard to his homosexuality, about which he was dangerously open. David's most famous paper, delivered at a conference in Zurich in 1933, was concerned with Cerf Beer and his own battles against prejudice of the Germanic elements of Strasbourg in a time when virtually no moral position was maintained and held.

The sole surviving photo of Gabriel David as an adult shows him sat at the table of a cafe, just past Quai des Pêcheurs, where many young academics from the university met to discuss and debate the latest topics of the day. His confident character is clear to see in the photograph, as is his famous umbrella which he purportedly never went anywhere without, such was the long stride of his walk which required some measure via the sharp placing of its metallic head onto the cobbles, as well as his known dislike of being even slightly dampened by rain or snow. He also had a fondness for pocket mirrors and certain stoned gems which he would wear as customised tiepins, including a famous amber-headed brooch which was said to have belonged to his mother. Gabriel David's anthropological work drew him great acclaim in the department and his desire to break into more popular, even journalistic writing on the history of the city was well noted. Also documented is the writer's stormy relationship with his father, who eventually betrayed both son and mother in the violent years of the Second World War. In 1939, over 100,000 people of all races, creeds and character were evacuated from the city with only a few hours to spare. Along with this exodus of people, the glass that made up the windows of the cathedral was taken out, sheathed in protective cases and stored safely by the town council. Still a great many people stayed, having known of their own city's turbulent past, being on the border between France and Germany and having traded hands violently between them several times. Unusually, in spite of knowing of the danger the Nazis posed to him due to his half-Jewish descent and his homosexuality, David stayed in the town, believing naively that he would survive via his infamous wit and charm. During the occupation by the Germans, Alsace as a whole became part of the *Gau Baden-Elsaß* or *Gau Oberrhein*

and under the jurisdiction of a certain Robert Wagner. Many
places and monuments that emphasised the city's French
character were deemed unsuitable by the ruling military. The
statue of General Kléber was removed and stored away just
like the delicate glass of the cathedral, hidden in the Musée
Historique; France was now in the past tense for the citizens
living in the Year Zero of the Third Reich. Even Kléber's
ashes, prominently returned to Strasbourg in previous years
to mark his achievements – his place of birth – and placed
in the base of the statue, were moved temporarily to the
cemetery in the Cronenbourg district; Place Kléber renamed
Karl Roos Platz, much to Gabriel David's amusement, who
loudly and publicly bad-mouthed the various changes
instigated by the occupiers. On one occasion, which David
supposedly witnessed, some local children were even
reported to the relevant authority when, during church,
they referred to their parson as *Abbé* rather than the German,
Pfarrer. Gabriel David was to fall on hard times, not least
because he had underestimated the danger he was to be put
in at the hands of the Nazis, his university life shielding him
somewhat, his head deep in his studies and not in the reality
around him. He had, so it was said, read too much into
Berlin's notorious image of previous years, and assumed his
dandyism would see him through the war. This was a new
war waged by a new, meticulous enemy. Many colleagues
from a variety of departments at the university were arrested
and deported, including the eminent physics professor
Charles Sadron who, when finally interred at the camp at
Mittelbau-Dora, sometimes known as Dora-Nordhausen,
convinced his captors that he had turned sides and spent
the remainder of the war secretly sabotaging the guidance

systems of V1 and V2 missiles. Gabriel David's relationship with his father, so it is said, grew more strained as it became apparent that David senior did not consider the love of his wife and son strong enough to put his own life and career in danger. Being apparently of non-Jewish descent himself, and in spite of his surname, Josef David eventually turned in both his wife and his son to the authorities (it is suggested that David senior somehow hid his own probable Jewish heritage in plain sight and attributed the heritage of his son to his wife). Gabriel David disappeared swiftly from the city, first thought to have been arrested by the Gestapo. It was only some months after that it was revealed he had tried to escape and had failed, his mother methodically shot while he was left to run into the surrounding countryside. Though Gabriel David himself was never officially designated as deceased, a report does suggest that one 'alien' attempting escape in one of the villages outside of the city was shot and killed; a photograph found in his pocket still survives to this day. It is suggested by some academics that the photo shows Madame David and a very young Gabriel David, in happier days before the circularity of their history came down upon them, though it has never been confirmed.

Josef David survived the war unmolested, but suffered after it. Strasbourg adopted a new identity card categorisation system after the fighting had ceased in order to help those who had suffered greatly at the hands of the occupiers. This meant each citizen was given a card demarcating A, B, C and D. Many German citizens like Josef David received a D classification, which was the lowest grade and meant work was incredibly difficult to find and maintain. It also

implied collusion with the enemy and unconsciously demarcated the traitors of the city. Applications for higher level categorisation were posted on a variety of noticeboards in Place du Château, where opportunities for French naturalisation were advertised and updated by the town's new authorities on a weekly basis. Josef David died of a brain haemorrhage caused by a blow to the head, received in a scuffle near these boards when one of his son's colleagues, never properly identified, recognised the traitorous man looking for the opportunity to be recognised as a French citizen and sought to take revenge for the death of his friend. The police report from the time has little detail, though it does suggest that Gabriel David's father was beaten to a bloody pulp with a stone pulled up from the ground, and several of his teeth were later found lying in between the cobbles by the investigating officers. The man's business was liquidated in a similar fashion to much of the archive of his son's work during the occupation, and his body was buried in an unmarked public grave outside of the city, said to be near the spot of one of the mass pits where many of the Jews were buried in the great plague massacre of 1349.

The German word *Fernweh* deserves some debate surrounding its meaning. In a literal translation into English, it comes across as a sickness, discomfort or pain (*Weh*) caused by a desire to be far away (*Fern*); a basic need to travel into the distance from a fixed point of home. With the amalgamation of the segments, the feeling the word induces is often attributed as some light inversion

of *Heimweh* or *Heimlich*, meaning 'homesickness'. Whereas
Heimweh signals a relatively normal preoccupation – the
longing to be back home when afar, at least in some basic
sense – *Fernweh* implies a striving forward, a desire to
wander away from home. It has been described as similar
to wanderlust, yet what if that desire for distance was
built on a need to escape, or even forcibly cut loose by
circumstance from home? It's an ideal that requires a
home in the first place to wander away from. While in
Strasbourg, I had been debating for some time, having
read about the term in a book of essays, whether I was in
the midst of a bout of minor *Fernweh*, yet my wandering
had frozen me in one place far away from a previous
home. I could not shake the feeling that I had, in fact,
stumbled upon a pessimistic cousin of *Fernweh*. Far from
being synonymic of wanderlust, a word which reminded
me of the travels of my partner – the sort of person who
would have wooden cut-outs of 'wanderlust' hanging on
kitchen walls – I had marooned myself in a place far from
where I lived. There needed to be, so I thought, a word
that described, not the desire to travel far from home
for joy, but instead the desire to travel away out of sheer
necessity. The divide between place and self had melted
at such a drastic and alarming level that journey was no
longer a feasible concept to describe my own state. Simply
being was enough of a preoccupation to consider a place,
rather than the need to have the possibility of a returning
momentum. My flat hardly counted as a home, more of a
room I let things happen in. All movement was instead
rendered as a lost meandering.

For my partner, travelling in what I assumed to be joyful

glee around South America in between medical studies, the journey's excitement lay in a change that would eventually resolve itself into a cadence of home. The forests and exotica of the southern reaches would eventually dissolve pleasantly, after a string of airports, bus stations and trains, back into the streets of Strasbourg with its cobbles, amber hues and its whispering history. *Fernweh*, on the other hand, turned into a genuine malady once finally removed from any sense of belonging, which I had accepted as being my normal state of mind for some years, even before my father's death. I could feel a sense of muddling as I continued to walk the streets of the city, in a permanent state of loss and refusing to acknowledge the demise of what I once knew as home back in Crystal Palace. The idea of enveloping myself in history and memorabilia worked incredibly well for most of the time, especially in the daytime, and my encounter with Brice had confirmed my need to know more.

I could sit for hours learning about Strasbourg. I read about how a guild of boatman in the 1800s had organised what could be described as a water jousting event on the Ill outside the Church of Saint-Guillaume, much to the amusement of the local crowds, whose cheers I swear I could sometimes hear. Yet in those fleeting moments before sleep, if sleep ever accepted its desperate welcome, my mind would become hyperactive with thoughts and images of my father, dead and hanging sodden from a tree, or worse, swaying from the pushes of the malicious Erl-King. I could no longer recall the jovial elements of water jousting on the Ill when lying in the dark. Instead, the information would turn against me. I would recall from the day's reading that, alongside this jousting, another game took place called *jeu de l'Oie* or the Goose Game or the Game

of the Goose. The game, so a paper I had read suggested in
detail, would involve a piece of rope tied over the Ill, held onto
the hooks of two buildings. Geese and birds in general would
be hung and tied to this rope, dead or alive. It reminded me
of the practice certain rural English farming communities had
of hanging dead moles on barbed wire after they have been
plucked from the muddy earth. Rather than being a marker for
how many had been killed, the birds would hang down over
the water while the town's youth, dressed in the traditional
baggy clothing of the period, would attempt to grab them.
The game seemed in poor taste but perfectly innocuous in the
daylight hours as I stared out of the flat's window towards
the cathedral and the river. But at night, the image took on
a horrific quality. I could hear the crowds that had gathered
near Quai Saint-Etienne by the Fossé du Faux-Rempart to
watch the spectacle, cheering as a young man snatched at the
air, weighed down and troubled by the dirty river water as
he tried in vain to pull sharply down upon the winding neck
of a swan. I would find myself standing with this crowd of
onlookers, making my way closer to the edge to get a better
view before a great roar from the spectators would rise into
the air, several of whom blocked my field of vision. In the
darkness of my room, I would see the Ill and its damp rope,
making my way through the crowd only to see my father's
lifeless body hanging there; a young boy snatching up at his
broken neck and trying to pull his limp corpse down into the
water as a deathly prize. I could not shake these visions, his
neck constantly dangling down in the dark or his body being
pulled into the Ill by a young *Strasbourgeois* wishing to claim
it for his supper or drag it underwater to render my father's
final contorted movements dead.

I was rootless now even though my father was, I hoped, deep in the ground, spreading permanently between other roots writhing within the earth and soil. I continued walking around the streets in those hoarfrost days as autumn faded, further along the river and back through the centre, always cutting along via the cathedral and finding myself on Rue du Vieux-Marché-aux-Poissons, which seemed to draw my stride towards it as if I was in search of something further that was not yet perceivable. It was while considering these problems, this illness and the reality of a sorrowful marooning, that I unusually began to consider the life of Johann Wolfgang von Goethe. On this road, almost opposite where Brice had his stall when I first spoke to him, a small plaque that I had barely noticed adorned the wall of a building. Further down from Gutenberg, a profile of Goethe, with carved information below it, suggested that the writer had lived there between the years of 1770 and 1771. The plaque was some way above the building's entrance, almost hidden in fact. I was not sure how I noticed the monument, hanging between the first and second floor of the building, now a luxury clothes shop.

The weather that month had been turning, with the end of the year soon approaching. A light mist often hung over the streets in the mornings, giving way to spates of rainfall and, on the rare occasion, fleeting sunlight. On the day I saw Goethe's head adorning the building, the streets were in their misty phase, soon to give way once more to rain. Goethe's building was an unusual burgundy colour, an aspect I couldn't help but notice standing out in a row of mostly yellow and grey buildings, as if the colour

designated some previous gruesome use for the building's
rooms, rather like the museum down the way which was
previously the city's abattoir. Its woodwork was painted an
ominous black, further adding to the Gothic nature of its
design while the plaque lay innocuously below a window,
resembling an emblem put out by local people during
elections to show support for a certain candidate or cause.
The period of time celebrated on the monument seemed so
short that I looked at the plaque a number of times, unsure
whether I was reading it properly, perhaps mistaking a
one for a seven. Though Goethe was born in Frankfurt and
learned a great deal while living there, so one of the many
essays on the man I read later suggested, his crumbling
relationship with his father and several severe illnesses
eventually led him to complete his studies in law at the
University of Strasbourg, if only to avoid the fate of all but
one of his siblings who had died at a young age. I imagined
what Goethe's tuition must have been like, occasioning
images of his father sternly trying to lecture him in Latin at a
small wooden table in a darkened Frankfurt room. Perhaps
I was being melodramatic. Strasbourg turned the Lutheran
Humanist German Gymnasium into a university in 1621,
specialising in medicine and law as well as several smaller
ventures into natural history and astronomy. Here Goethe
continued his studies, though it was hard to imagine this as
a suitable background for a poet.

Having found another figure to consider, I immediately
made my way back to the flat to find out more about the
poet and writer. I had only read *Faust* once, the epic work
that Goethe was arguably most famed for, at least in Britain.
I had read it naively as a teenager, when such books held a

level of cultural value outside of their basic qualities. Being seen reading it was just as important as reading it, such were those naive days. I recalled also reading broadsheets in the same manner and respecting the opinions of their writers, equally holding a sort of exotic sway, long since dissipated thanks to the unavoidably hollow reality of so much of their writing. I could not, so I admitted to myself while turning once more onto the familiar cobbles of Grand'Rue, remember virtually anything about Goethe's book. Most of the images I associated with him were derived from a silent film version of the story I had seen some years previous with my partner, albeit against his will as he, by his own admission, only liked American comedies and things he could 'switch off' to. It was directed by F.W. Murnau and worked well on the big screen, so much so that my partner bought me a DVD of it for a later birthday with an unusual woodcut design on its cover, nicer than my teenage paperback edition in fact. As the director had also made the famous unauthorised adaptation of Bram Stoker's *Dracula* in the form of *Nosferatu*, I knew that I was also mistaking images from this overly Gothic and horrific film for Goethe's images; Mephistopheles now turned inaccurately into the dreadful, vampiric count in my mind's eye.

I wanted to take the route back through Grand'Rue in order to pick up a *kugelhopf*, an Alsatian speciality whose unusually organised shape, with segments like the folded petals of a flower, made it ideal for an easily planned series of breakfasts in the week. I had taken to eating very little since my father's suicide, my body dropping away beneath my clothes, and so the easiest of meal options, especially meals that arranged their portions themselves, so to speak,

had a unique draw during my time in Strasbourg. There
was a bakery I had taken to visiting, possessed of a warm
glow almost always emanating from its large window, and
I soon came upon it as bikes travelled by incredibly close
and quickly. I learned while my partner was here that a
queue was always to be expected at this bakery due to its
popularity, even early in the morning. Luckily, so I thought,
the queue was minimal and provided just enough time to
admire the cakes and pastries that the bakery specialised in.
There lay in front of me a huge variety of different sized
bretzels – whose history and esoteric shape was as much a
mystery as Gutenberg's time in the city – a sort of human-
shaped brioche called *männele*, a variety of colourful pies
adorned with delicious looking fruit that glistened under
the bright light of the glass display cabinet, and what I had
come for, a variety of different sized *kugelhopf.* The pastry is
an unusual shape that suggests some vortex sitting within
its orderly fingers and around its protruding base. Cutting
into it, I had found on previous occasions, felt blasphemous,
destroying a perfect order produced by the golden ratio. I
ordered the largest one from the old woman at the counter
and thought how, due to the exact nature of the pastry's
shape, all the smaller options that sat in small groups on
a wooden shelf implied a Russian doll effect, almost as if
a number of cakes could be contained within the large one
that I was buying.

I remembered the unusual feeling that always
accompanied me when walking around Crystal Palace
carrying food in my hands rather than in bags, the
discomfort being unexplainable yet part of the English
malady; a total rejection of life on an intuitive level, instead

calculating every precise movement and word in the hope of being seen a certain way. Englishness was akin to the feeling my skeleton sometimes had of wanting to fold my own body in upon itself to avoid all sense of the world. But I had quickly grown used to being one of the many in Strasbourg who partook in the daily ritual of carrying baguettes, cakes and extravagant pastries around by hand, just as the English carry umbrellas and laptops and fear. I felt happy to be carrying this *kugelhopf* in its small brown bag under my arms, noticing the dark patterns that the grease from its dough was making through the paper. I wondered then if Goethe had eaten *kugelhopf* during his stay here, and recognised how enjoyably trivial my mind had become since my father's death and my stony silence towards my mother's barrage of insulting messages, now taking place online and through snide updates to her various social pages, as well as the more personal text messages.

I was almost at the end of Grand'Rue in Petite France and near the flat when I saw a familiar face. I actually heard this familiar presence before seeing him, as he was always accompanied by a small set of speakers playing a variety of heavy metal music at loud volumes, especially in summer when I had first met the man in question. His name, so he told me once when I had given him some change, was Michel, and I knew little else about him other than he was homeless, an alcoholic and a fan of heavy metal. We had chatted briefly but regularly, much to the surprise of the locals and my partner, who, out of paranoia, often warned me off talking to any men here. Michel was always to be seen wearing his leather waistcoat over a small variety of band T-shirts, ragged and ripped jeans and large black boots, no matter what the weather. I had always expressed a quiet appreciation for the man's earnestness if only because his begging sign, which had yet to change since first seeing him in Grand'Rue on my first visit to the city, read quite simply 'A euro for a drink please!' in French. He would sit on the steps of shops listening to his music, sometimes wandering into the centre of the street to bow to passers-by and ask for change, though, if he had a bottle or two already bought, he would simply sit in some doorway or perched on a front step quite happily listening and drinking the day away. Michel was stood in the centre of the street on this day, his music playing loudly while he waved his long black hair at elderly women and young children. He spotted me instantly and cried out, 'Ahh! The Duchess!' It was a name he had christened me with as soon as he had first heard my English accent attempting to speak French. I stopped and he noticed the *kugelhopf* underneath my arm, congratulating me on my choice. I could hear the music and returned the compliment, recognising an English band that I had listened to when younger. He asked what I had been doing, though I doubted whether he was really interested. It was simply patter for more small change or food, I thought. But I told him at any rate of my interest in the history of Strasbourg and how I was on my way back to the flat to read about Goethe, who had lived further down the road on Rue du Vieux-Marché-aux-Poissons. He seemed genuinely interested; his false character having been easy to spot in previous conversations, as his English did not stretch far enough for deception. 'Goethe?' he asked. 'I read him ages ago. There's a German band that use his poems,' he said. 'I think, *un moment*,' and he wandered back to pull out a notebook from a small leather satchel he had hidden in a pile of items comprising of empty cans of drink, a small pile of CDs, some tattered items of clothing and some coat-hangers.

He came back and showed me the small book, opening it at the first page, which was astonishing to look at. On the paper there were small blocks of writing almost in micro-script, neatly arranged into squares the size of coasters. The book resembled a stamp collection or family photo album of sorts, such was its neatness, only made of tiny notes and handwriting rather than images. The words, from what I could see, were a mixture of English, French and German, though I could not make out what they said at first. 'This,' Michel continued, 'is my lyric book. Sometimes, if I hear a lyric I – err, like, yes – like, then I write it here. I sometimes write my own too, but I always have so much to do,' he said with a wry smile. The book had taken me completely by surprise, being so organised in stark contrast to its seemingly chaotic owner whose pile of belongings resembled a piece of contemporary art. He began to turn the pages looking for something. 'Now,' he began, 'there is a lyric somewhere,' he said with the dramatic flair of a studious librarian. I began to feel conspicuous stood in the middle of the street with Michel and I could feel the eyes of strangers burning into us. Perhaps, so I thought, they believed they were witnessing an act of kindness or, more likely, a potential sale of drugs. In reality, the man was showing me what I assumed to be his most prized possession, but I was still unsure as to why. Desiring to break the silence and stillness between us on the foggy road, I pulled the top part of the *kugelhopf* out of its wrapping and ripped a piece of it off, handing it to Michel whose face opened into a smile of gratitude. Taking the piece, he continued riffling through the volume while eating until he came to a page and then, crying 'Aha!' loudly, he handed me the book and began to talk in between chewing. 'This lyric I am sure, great band, was taken from *Erlkönig*.' I looked down on the page that seemed nothing less than a collection of scurrying ants. His finger pointed to the small box of intricate writing on the top left of the page and I looked towards it, trying to read the tiny writing. The lyric was in German and clearly mentioned '*der König aller Winde*'.

'It's not exact but it's about the same thing... the old folk story, yes,' Michel said. I could not recall the poem other than as a brief fragment from a Franz Schubert *Lied* I had studied as an undergraduate when music, rather than history, was my subject, but I was still impressed generally at the man's shared desire for the archaic. This was when I finally knew that the shroud I had seen was from shadow worlds beyond rather than illness, formed from all those glimpses of images of this fantastical creature, a creature of forests and children's nightmares. I asked if I could write down the words in my phone, or at least take a photo so I could search for them later online. Michel seemed incredibly pleased at the prospect that he had helped me, so I bent down with the book balanced on my knees while I angled the photograph onto my phone, fighting against the shaking of my legs which had begun to shiver from standing still. I handed the book back and thanked him, noticing that, having been holding the *kugelhopf* since I had taken the book, Michel had been gradually helping himself to more of the pastry in large ripped handfuls of dough, his T-shirt covered in crumbs while several raisins lay in between the cobbles in front of me. 'You can have it,' I said to him, paying for the interesting distraction with pastry; goods for goods. I bid farewell to Michel and he wandered back to his spot by his speakers, putting the book carefully underneath the pile of things, turning the music up even louder than it was before while continuing to pick at the cake. I wanted to know more about the *Erlkönig* – 'fairy king' in English – from this moment on, who was now very much the Erl-King rather than merely a shroud. Curiosity isn't, perhaps, quite the right word, just as wanderlust wasn't the right word. I was haunted by the Erl-King, the shadows, the figures, the shrouds, the slight movements down street corners: it had been him, unleashed by my father's self-inflicted violence in Crystal Palace. He was following, desiring flesh, feasting and strengthening on the sadness of his victim. That an image could travel from folklore, through to Goethe and then to the lyrics of a modern metal band felt like a profound journey, but also induced fear. This thing could travel across barriers of culture and language and time.

The mist was lifting as I returned to Rue du Cygne and I knew that I would have to spend the rest of the day looking up information about Goethe's poem rather than *Faust*. The sun gradually shone through the windows, soon lifting the mist from the ground, and I watched a group of people with a ladder some way back into Petite France adorn a restaurant with a variety of large Christmas decorations. The festive period was soon approaching, and I had all but ignored the other signs of its impending arrival. It was obvious why: Christmas would imply family and family implied death, my harridan mother, England sinking, and the things I wished to banish. But my mind was preoccupied with other things and I was thankful that the only people I would usually buy things for were either dead, disowning me or travelling around South America. *You always manage to ruin Christmas, Isabelle, haven't you heard of freedom of speech?* I searched through the cupboards looking for a substitute for the *kugelhopf* that Michel had commandeered, before sitting down to research. It was a difficult task, if only because I had underestimated how much had actually been written about Goethe. I found one particular website that had a brief history of his years in the city and his time at university where, so it said, Goethe had fallen for the landscape all around the department and in particular for the Cathedral of Our Lady, the Virgin. I noticed that, of the list of things that Goethe discovered in this brief period of excited exploration, alongside The Bible, Shakespeare, Homer and Johann Gottfried Herder, the writer had become interested in the many folk songs of the region and elsewhere. I found a recording of the Schubert *Lied* and remembered the only aspect I could of the lecture I had sat in upon several years previous; that the music of the piano is said to resemble the rumblings of an old horse-drawn cart bumping along a country road while the father, whose son sings many passages from the poem, all but ignores the potential seduction and abduction of the boy by the ethereal presence of the elfin king. The father lost his son, unaware, or perhaps the son lost his father. Herder, so another paper said, had actually popularised the term '*Erlkönig*' in print in his poetic ballad, *Erlkönigs Tochter*, in 1778. It all seemed intricately connected on the cultural map of my stay, all tributaries leading to the one truth I was doing my best to avoid. Based on the Danish legend of an elfin being who ensnares people, especially children, to satisfy a variety of needs, lustful and vengeful, I had underestimated how dark the folklore actually was. It resembled more a modern crime thriller rather than an old tale told around the fire. Herder himself arrived in Strasbourg in 1770, the year Goethe arrived at the university. The two had met and, so I thought, the older writer seemed a cultural father figure of sorts being a few years older, introducing Goethe to a variety of works and ideas, including the folk legends that had already fascinated Herder enough to produce several poetic works and ballads. I used an algorithm to translate the original Herder poem in German, one line standing out in particular. It read:

> *Hör' an, mein Sohn, sag' an mir gleich,*
> *Wie ist dein' Farbe blaß und bleich?*

The program translated it as, 'Listen, my son, tell me right away, how is your colour paler and paler?' The words had an unusual effect upon my mind, the word 'paler' in particular seeming to drain the colour from the room. I looked down at my hands stretched over a dirty keyboard and found my scarred skin to be almost translucent, my eyes aching as if they were slowly going blind. It was as though I was held by blindness at a distance from a majestic secret that could not be shared. Herr Oluf of the poem ends up dead in the forest, desiring his pale bride, having spurned the daughter of the *Erlkönig* who offered him gold and riches on his way to be married. I was envious; the Erl-King was more confident in those days. He barely showed himself now,

the coward, except under a mantle of ambiguity. Perhaps
the sanctimony of affection led only down this pale path,
lit occasionally as if seen through the leaking sap of trees
or through rays of sunlight, shining rarely on winter days.
I had walked the road named after the poet, Rue Herder,
some months previous when lost after a day's walk around
Parc de l'Orangerie near the European Parliament. It housed
the Swiss Consulate and, so I remembered, little else. I could
picture Herder and Goethe talking together in the grassy
pastures of the university, debating Homer and other things
that must have distracted the younger student of law from
his growing antipathy towards his father back in Frankfurt.
It was clear that Herder did indeed act as an important
figure for Goethe, imbuing him with enough interest and
confidence to begin writing his own poems, later released
anonymously as the volume *Annette* in 1770.

These early poems lacked the darkness that I was
looking for, the presence of the *Erlkönig* and other
maladies of the mind. I needed writing that shared our
muted vision, our morbid gaze. Instead, the poems I found
from his time in Strasbourg were love-struck, seemingly
dedicated to the daughter of a parson, Friederike Brion,
whom Goethe had met in a parsonage in Sessenheim, a
small area in the Bas-Rhin further north of Strasbourg
near Haguenau. They were poems doused with affection
and felt alien; the possible overlap with or application
to my own relationship having since disappeared. The
daughter was, so I thought, a physical embodiment of the
region, cast off when the writer returned to Frankfurt.
There was no sense of *Fernweh* for the writer, however.
His time in Strasbourg, so another paper suggested, was

filled with wandered imaginings, ghost-stepping after this young woman, and concluded that the city had been a rebirth of sorts. But, with all this information, I still could not shake the visions of the *Erlkönig* and so began to read a translation of the poem, arguably far more effective than the first response written by Herder. Goethe's final stanza continued to rumble on just like the piano in Schubert's *Lied*:

> *The father shudders, his ride is wild,*
> *In his arms he's holding the groaning child,*
> *Reaches the court with toil and dread.*
> *The child he held in his arms was dead.*

The father had totally failed the child. That was my first thought; having ignored his son's pleas for help, he had lost him. The thought pushed my eyes towards the window, the sky stretched out over the buildings in front of me, a great celestial geometry hidden by the clouds of that typical Strasbourg day. I imagined the father's guilt, blackened with the hunger to reach his destination, now turned rotten and coursing through his body like a ghastly poison. I could not shake the feeling that I myself had been followed since staying here, as if the *Erlkönig*, even before I knew it was he, had ordained my seduction and ultimate demise since my father had committed his last act. I recalled the feeling of being followed while walking along the river, the compulsion to look over my shoulder, as if a whispering malevolence had descended from the heights of the cathedral and followed me back on dark winter nights to Rue du Cygne. The thought took possession of my hindsight, imbuing each memory of lonely walking with a new, unseen presence, the malevolent Erl-King and his potential deathly pleasures.

I decided that it was best for now to stop looking into the life of Goethe in Strasbourg. I had found much of interest, but the fragility of my own mental state was becoming clear. Of all things, I required a walk, but night was descending quickly over the town and I had little compulsion to allow the *Erlkönig*, hovering through the streets of the city, to try and acquire another being for his delectation, at least at first. Before closing the laptop, checking various notifications and confused emails from new colleagues asking again for me to explain my absence, and attempting to consider what I was to eat, I noticed that Goethe had further monuments built and dedicated to him in town. The tourist website that the search engine had brought up suggested that there were in fact two further monuments to the writer in the university sector, a picture of one in particular looking daunting and impressive. Making a brief note of where they were, I closed the lid on the blue light of the screen, realising for the first time that, having been sat in the room for the rest of the day, I had failed to notice the sun fully descending and darkness flooding into the room. The lights had come on over the various buildings of Petite France, indicating with the accuracy of a clock that night had arrived. Red lights flashed on the main bridge while the long building of the Barrage Vauban was lit with an assortment of colours, the towers of Petite France now an ominous green.

That night, the *Erlkönig* encircled the room. I soon gave way to his presence, allowing him in, letting him swallow me whole; 'fly through the window and take me, devour me whole,' I thought, if only to be rid of this heaviness within. I felt the creature drift towards the bed, taking his pleasure from my body, pulverising me into the mattress as his frame engulfed me. His long fingers stretched out over my torso, the light swallowed by his writhing body as I felt him grind my essence down. In the depths of his ecstasy, I would share only that final second of destruction, that moment when the confusing pleasures of the touch from his spindly hands and pointed body would draw a final breath from my lungs, my lower half thrusting into the air to catch that little death. I would finally rejoin my father, if only for an instant. I saw him, the Erl-King, tearing me in two down the middle, breaking against me again and again, my legs high in the air like when my partner was in the mood, representing that first break in my body; that snap towards a hopeful pleasure. I hoped, begged even, for an end, chasing the destruction. Gather my torn teeth, my broken ribs, scrunched legs and cries of resisting desire, I thought; take them and *go*.

The flashing of the safety light on the Ponts Couverts seemed particularly stark when alone again, leaving these moments behind; my body breathless, sweating and hollow. Sometimes the room was lit with Morse code as I felt the sweat on my body from its previous movements and spasms. I wondered, once I had recovered from this visitation, what Goethe had thought of the area, now renowned as a tourist attraction that filled daily with buses of people documenting each brick and stone with phones and cameras. I had taken to noticing the area's characters, not least Farid with his weekend car parking business. I had never spoken to Farid but admired his bravado whenever witnessing it, learning his name from my partner's father.

An Algerian immigrant, he appeared most weekends, directing cars to the rare and much sought-after spaces for visitors, then asking for change in exchange for his services. His brother, whose name I never learned, operated the same business in a car park just off Grand'Rue, though seemed less inconspicuous due to his predilection for wearing a large Mexican sombrero and an extravagant studded belt, looking like an extra from an old Hollywood Western. Often, there was a musician who practised around Petite France too. His reasons, however, were not driven by finance. I first noticed him in the summer when the sound of an old recorder filled the air, providing the surreal feeling of falling back through time. Behind one of the large towers sat upon the Ponts Couverts, the musician would often slump against the wall or sit on the edge overlooking the water while playing. When practising the wooden recorder, the bridge and the surrounding architecture gained qualities which I could not fully describe, except to say that they felt more alive. At other times, the musician – a young man in tattered clothing and almost always wearing a maroon woollen hat no matter the weather – would be playing more recognisable music on an alto saxophone. The windows of the flat could be opened wide on summer days so that the jazz melodies would float in with the air. The design of the Barrage Vauban and Ponts Couverts seemed to attract such characters, sometimes there for the more obvious reason of busking: men with dreadlocks making large bubbles with sticks plunged into a bucket of soapy water, and a violin player who seemed to only have the ability to repeat certain segments of Vivaldi's *Spring* over and over, as well as some general beggars who would sit with signs detailing hunger and dependent family members, though less blunt than Michel's sign on Grand'Rue. I stood up to look out of the window after yet another vision of my father's hanging body had brushed away the light sleep I had fallen into, staring down onto the roads at night, imagining the Erl-King leaping from the window to steal pleasure from the next victim, willing or otherwise. The old hunched woman who regularly begged in the area could be seen from the window, hobbling along the bridge once more, out surprisingly late. My thoughts turned to Michel, who I hoped was warm and still savouring some of his *kugelhopf*. The old beggar woman disappeared, and I thought perhaps the elfin king had come and whisked her away too as I got back into bed, a fresh glass of water now by the lamp. The leaves had by then fallen from the area's many trees. 'In withered leaves, the night-wind blows,' just as Goethe had once written, one of the few things I could remember from his work. I woke early the following morning, feeling the bags beneath my eyes drag my head down towards the ground, as if I had been up all night with a new lover, not yet stale from repetition.

It was still an ungodly hour, I thought, though not the hour of the Erl-King or the sleeping moments when his emissaries stalked the streets in search of future bounty for their king. I noticed, looking out of the window, however, that several police officers were on the main entrance at the start of the Ponts Couverts. Something my partner had told me when we had last messaged played upon my mind. The men were setting up what appeared to be a barrier made of steel mesh, several others walking through the Barrage Vauban who were, so I assumed, setting up another cordon on the other side of the building in Place Jean-Hans Arp. The men had alarming looking rifles slung over their shoulders and it was only later that I realised what this presence meant: the beginning of the Christmas Market. I had been so lost in thought while wandering, so determined to see backwards rather than face the present, that I had failed to question why a large number of small wooden sheds had started to line the streets. The day was breaking quickly, and the tourists were beginning to flock, their coaches arriving and rumbling outside the building. I developed a certain voyeurism in watching the groups of these tourists whose coaches parked along the road underneath Rue du Cygne as the hours drew on. They would make their way through the cordon and submit themselves to being searched, forced at great annoyance to empty large bags. All the while, I was drinking coffee to lighten the heaviness in my mind along with a few cigarettes, and looking on with a malevolent glee not unlike that of the *Erlkönig* himself. I was thankful as I knew my destination today would not require me to cross the cordon which I presumed, like the last few years, would cover every entrance to the main island of Strasbourg around the canals leading off from the Ill.

The towers of Petite France, the *Heinrichsturm*, the *Hans von Altheimturm* and the 'French Tower', were again reflecting their defensive position of centuries past, though the main defence in years previous seems to have been against an invasion from a variety of venereal diseases in those early days of the sixteenth century, said to be originating from the French in the area. The phrase '*zum Franzosen*' or 'to the French' designating the Hospice des Vérolés that made up a large part of the area, where many of the infected French were isolated, and is said to be the origin of the name Petite France; syphilis being named *Franzosenkrankheit* or the French Disease. My partner often took great delight in telling me this. I imagined the shame of being sent there, to Petite France, locked into rooms with hay on the floor while a variety of irritations spread through already battered genitalia. I laughed at the tourists' eagerness to get in to this space, wondering whether they knew what they were photographing. The beautiful area whose poetry was obvious in the name alone, *La Petite France*; did they know they were walking over the isolation site for those ravaged by venereal infection, probably brought over from the ports of Naples and the military who travelled from there? The point was more amusing when spotting newlyweds throughout the year, couples who had travelled far for the sole purpose of having their wedding photos taken in a clichéd cornucopia of romantic European surroundings. All, so I would regularly think, built on the memory of infection. The infection of memory is perhaps more apt. *We have done so much for you, and you act like you achieved it all by yourself, naïve brat.* I wanted to see the statues of Goethe that day, not being especially captivated by the small plaque on the house in Rue du Vieux-Marché-aux-Poissons. The university quarter where the other statues stood was some way along the banks of the water, turning off Quai des Pêcheurs and into the university's gardens and buildings. I hadn't wandered near there before except for a few days when walking further along towards the European Parliament buildings, Parc de l'Orangerie and Rue Herder, all in the sweltering heat of a pleasant month when my partner was here; long before his travels or the growing frost of our relationship. I thought of how much easier things were with him then, partly built from our ignorance of each other, still learning about each other's pleasures and limits. It was far from the grey tedium of where we were in the days before he left; manifesting in awkwardness even as we said goodbye at the train station, which had felt merely like saying goodbye before another day of work. I thought it was deliberate on his part, but it was hard to tell, as he openly admitted that he performed for me sometimes in order to keep some sense of mystery.

The weather was turning cold quickly, and so I dressed and made sure I was suitably wrapped up in woollen clothing and with an umbrella hanging naively out of my coat pocket. It was a wise decision for, only a little way alongside the water on Quai Saint-Nicolas, a light drizzle of rain turned into an icing sugar coating of snow. It drove the few people outside into nearby cafes or under the covered walkways of the more modern buildings that overstretched the pavements of Rue de la Division Leclerc and Rue de la 1ère Armée with a makeshift roof. I took note whenever I could of the windows of the shops that lay on the riverside, many of which were old curiosity and antique shops. I thought of Brice's father, trying like his father before him to find Gutenberg's mirror, and in the first of several mistaken glances I could have sworn that some mirrored object reflected from a number of different windows. In a shop window on Quai des Bateliers, a similarly shining object seemed hidden underneath an array of bric-a-brac. There were piles of old books, several plates detailing traditional Alsatian designs, some dolls with their clothes faded and dirty, a sea of jewelled trinkets giving the impression of one great, textured mass by their tiny corresponding price labels written in flowing handwriting, a chipped vase that had what looked to be a painting by Monet cheaply stretched over its shaping, and a small wooden medallion that had a three-dimensional portrait of General Kléber in its centre with the years '1753 –1800' carved above the general's head. The flash of a reflected mirror, emitting rays caught from a holy relic perhaps, disappeared and I could not figure out where the item was in the array of antiquities. It seemed to have vanished once more, or perhaps it was a trick of the light caused by the increasingly heavy snowfall; a snowflake falling close enough to my eye to dazzle it. My mind then turned to General Kléber, who was himself born in Strasbourg and who I had looked up the week before after noticing his name in the main square of the town. The architect turned soldier was one of the generals of the Revolutionary Wars before he was assassinated by a Syrian student while out on the Egyptian campaign of 1799. I had seen his statue in Place Kléber, itself something that took over twenty years to find its placement in the square, so a tourist website had said. The area was only so named once the statue was built in 1840, the man's body having been brought back into the country when Louis XVIII had finally allowed its return from its distant burial on the Île d'If, a prison island more commonly known as Château d'If. Like my body kept within the self-imposed prison island of central Strasbourg, Kléber had been kept on his island due to the return of his body carrying potentially worrying symbolic meaning for revolutionaries. Kléber's heart was separated and buried in a dusty urn beneath the altar of the Saint-Louis Chapel in Les Invalides. The Syrian student of theology, Soleyman El-Halaby, was publicly executed in Cairo, impaled and burnt out of existence in a long, agonising and public death. I wandered further, thinking of this student, picturing his flesh and muscles slowly stripped to the bone by flame, but also giving consideration to Goethe too. I couldn't help but imagine, as I continued to walk, a still from the silent film version of *Faust* that I had seen; a title card that simply said '*Liebe*' surrounded by flaming, God-like rays. The power of the transcendent surrounding earthly life, perhaps. What did Soleyman El-Halaby perceive as his arms were burnt off, as his body was impaled and the public of Cairo watched?

The snow fell heavily and my journey into the university quarter was long and more difficult than I had anticipated due to the weather, continually slipping on the pavement as my shoes had a smooth sole. The snow was falling in thick clouds by then, the leather of my shoes rendered black with water as I traipsed through the slush; the cobbles and stone now almost totally hidden. Perhaps Soleyman El-Halaby saw the transcendent through the flames, like in the film. I hoped that he was blinded before his death, so as not to witness the full horrors that were befalling the rest of his body, sensed only by searing white pain. The buildings fell away into trees before a complicated road layout unfolded. The two towers of the Saint-Paul Reformed Church stood above the dead branches, and they looked more Gothic in the snow than they had done in the summer. The church had been damaged by Allied bombing during the Second World War but looked pristine, its complicated rose windows still perceivable in the minor snowstorm. I stood on the Pont d'Auvergne, admiring it for as long as my nose could take the cold. After a brief look at the freezing, high-level water flowing underneath the bridge, I wandered to my main destination. The road was wide, and it took some time to find Goethe's statue. It was only when realising that the statue and its small spit of land now acted as a roundabout for the traffic that I discovered where it was. I could see three figures through the white-out of the snow, the oxidised metal darkening their silhouettes. I hadn't considered the possibility of three statues, expecting there to be only one, and I wondered whether I was at the right place. It was at Place de l'Université and the statue, as I got closer, did seem to resemble portraits I had seen of Goethe, the grainy scans of paintings and drawings online, often covered with trademarks from photographic licensing websites. I was in the right place, the writer looking out over the vista of roads and trees rendered deathly by the weather. The statue itself, compared to the architecture which surrounds it, is not especially old. It was made by the Berlin sculptor Ernst Waegener in 1901 to commemorate Goethe's time at the university. Though there had been, so a promotional website stated, several Nobel Prize-winners produced by the university, Goethe is undoubtedly its most famous graduate. On Goethe's right sat *Melmonene*, the muse of tragedy, once the muse of chorus and melody. On his left sat *Polymnie* or Polymnia, the muse of lyric poetry. I wasn't sure what the combination of these figures said about Goethe. Perhaps the tragedy of Faust himself rather than the poet was being suggested. Ironically, Polymnia is the muse carrying the harp rather *Melmonene*, now reduced to a tragic figure rather than the giver of chorus. I cleared a little patch on the steps that descended from the statues, further soaking the leather of my damp shoes and sat looking up at the figures, trying to find some meaning. Nothing was coming, but I noticed that the snow had covered the sides of the statue and stood up to uncover them with my gloved hands.

There were two depictions on its sides that I imagined were ignored by passers-by even in good weather. They were certainly imperceptible when seen from a passing car window. The first showed Goethe falling in love with Friederike Brion in Sessenheim, the woman seated as Goethe stood reading from a volume, probably of his own work. It was a mirrored relationship, I thought, recalling my own partner insisting on reading out medical jargon while deliberately showing me gruesome photos of illnesses and injuries, knowing that my stomach would turn. The woman was sat in the same poise as the muses and the connection felt more complete; that really, the two muses were simply phantoms or even doubles of Brion, the inspiration for early attempts at poetry, the tragedy being his departure from Strasbourg to begin a life of law back in Frankfurt. He had left her behind; we were the same in that we had left our responsibilities to people in the distance. The other depiction was more unusual, showing Goethe standing on a platform of sorts clearly giving a speech. I failed to fully understand the image at first until I saw the rays of sunlight shining down on small, quaint houses whose rooftops could just be seen below the platform. The poet was stood on the rooftop of the cathedral, giving a reading or, more likely, simply declaring his love for the city with the excellent view no doubt commanded from up on high. It must have been an even more overpowering experience before the age of high-rise buildings.

Thoughts of my father had surfaced on and off for some time on this walk, my drowning of his death in history working to relative success, but not totally. Something about this particular image brought back memories of him; his shouting voice as I distracted him from his painting, the worry in my mother's face as yet another bill came in – his promises as messy and convoluted as the array of colours covering his hands and mixing palette. The image on the statue was optimistic and joyful. But nothing could shake the images building in my mind's eye of the past, of Crystal Palace and its view over the whole of London. I could picture my father looking on a sunny day down Gypsy Hill towards the whole of the city, with its increasing folly of sky-scraping buildings, basking in the view, which he would paint several times. Perhaps he even gulped in this view before walking further down the hill on the other side of the triangle, towards the park with its forest, filled with sturdy trees and many hanging branches. Dangling and sodden, he was back in my thoughts. *Don't you want to come back and see your handiwork, Isabelle?* The snow continued to fall, and I was on the verge of being snow-blind, in reality and memory, I considered walking to see the other supposed bust of Goethe, further into the campus down a road that was also named after him. The writer seemed to be the literal spine of the university. But in those moments of walking in the appalling weather, my skin felt as if it was burning and I decided not to face down the breeze. At first, I assumed that it was some effect of the deathly cold blowing over from the river and curving round with a certain malevolent agency, the breeze from the cloak of the *Erlkönig* as he flew gently past towards another victim. Perhaps he would be diverted and take me here on the wet stone. But, removing a glove and checking the skin of my face with a grey-looking hand, littered with prominent blue veins and scratches, I felt the warmth of tears running down my cheeks. I had been unaware of crying, the feeling of *Fernweh* driving forward my wandering to the point of sitting with the homeless Goethe and his muses alone in the snow but numb through a lack of a return. There was no real home for either of us, just a room at Rue du Cygne in Petite France that now failed to shield my own body from the *Erlkönig* who roamed the streets at night. I liked calling the Erl-King by his German title; it seemed more fitting, as if the English deformed and undermined his true power and touch. It was then time to return and, trying my best not to slip upon the treacherous ground, I made my way slowly back along the banks of the Ill. It was heavy going and I thought constantly of how little I had been distracted by my search for the statue and the muses, as if on this occasion it had actually made things worse.

Coming back to the strange square opposite my partner's apartment, I found myself drawn to a shop in Place Henri-Dunant. The square was chiefly a car park, one of the car parks where Farid often directed people to spaces in the hope of getting change in return. On a small patch of grass separating the tarmac of the car park from the cobbles of the Ponts Couverts, there sat a small bust of Henri Dunant, the Swiss businessman born in Geneva who, among other things, co-founded the Red Cross and was the recipient of the first Nobel Peace Prize in 1901. Later on, when searching quickly for further information about the man, I was struck by a particular section of his life, not because of anything specific that occurred in it but how the page had labelled it. It was simply called Dunant's 'Return to public memory', and I still cannot quite consider what this means other than the possible existence of a society's collective memories, linked together like a single gestalt entity. I was not, however, drawn to the statue of Dunant at this point, which was all but hidden underneath snow. Instead, there was a warm glow coming from a small shop next to a cafe behind the bust. I had only ever noticed the cafe before that day, never the shop, the two businesses sharing a strange doorway which hid the more introverted emporium. This was to be my first visit to the shop, from which I would buy my postcards. There was a light on within the window that was so warm and inviting that I felt how I assumed moths first feel when catching sight of some distant bulb or candle on a cold evening. In the window was a wealth of images, old pictures and postcards detailing all sorts of scenarios from forgotten times. Place d'Austerlitz, Pont du Corbeau, Rue du Vieux-Marché-aux-Poissons and many others could be seen from just a glance, and I would make sure to buy a great number of postcards on later ventures to the shop, unable to resist mementos. Heading in straight away through the strangely angled door, an old man met me with his gaze, surprised, if anything, that he had a customer in this weather. I learned on later visits that his name was Éric and I soon grew used to his gentle demeanour, formed behind thin glasses and a white moustache. In the shop were rows and rows of postcards contained in long wooden boxes, some specific – with labels detailing places, themes and people – some general, alongside larger cardboard boxes of old war photos, maps, large volumes of incredibly old texts, vintage documents that were probably considered important and far from detritus when first drawn up, old newspapers and a wall of further wooden boxes labelled as to the photographic contents held within. I greeted Éric, who probably thought that I simply wanted to take shelter from the weather, especially as I assumed his usual clientele to be, more than likely, much older than me. On future visits I would feel like his only real customer, never seeing another soul in the shop other than his own ghostly figure sat at a desk poring over various paraphernalia in sepia.

Flicking through the many photographs and postcards, I felt like I was walking through an older Strasbourg, the city that I could partly see behind the new American businesses and the garish new cars. I could see places I had visited and walked regularly but through an older vision. I considered buying some, but noticing that the price was higher for the postcards detailing inner-city Strasbourg, I began to explore elsewhere in the shop, promising that I would buy them in the future to map my own memory of this period in time. I wasn't sure what I was looking for during that visit but then I thought that, to make up for my cowardliness in failing to see the other statue of Goethe, I should perhaps look for a postcard of the square where his statue sat. Éric was surprised by the specificity of my request – '*Avez-vous des cartes postales de Johann Goethe?*' – but he seemed to know instantly where he could find something suitable. He pulled out two postcards from an old drawer, kept in plastic sheaths for their protection. They both showed the statue of Goethe I had just visited rather than the bust I had failed to see. The first picture showed the full monument, Goethe and his two muses standing so unaware of each other that all three characters looked as if they had just concluded a huge row, which had now resulted in the potential *ménage*-à-*trois* ignoring each other in the most cartoonish of fashions.

The trees behind looked thinner and I considered whether the monument had been more prominent a public place when not used as a slipway for the traffic. The plate on the sculpture showing Goethe standing on the rooftop of the cathedral was facing the camera too, but it could not be made out in the picture. Admittedly, it was only marginally better than my own snow-blind viewing, my eyesight faded by the sharp frost.

The second postcard showed Goethe alone, with his muses rejected and left outside of the frame like spurned lovers or parents who, having split-up, carefully and methodically crop their old family photos with scissors to avoid the association between their failed relationship and their offspring. Such an action never works, it never hides the failure. *You may as well have tied the rope around his neck personally, Isabelle.* The day in this photograph seemed much warmer and, on inspecting the date, it was clear that the postcard was produced very close to the time when the monument was first built and fashioned. At Goethe's feet were a range of flowers and wreaths, as if the author had only recently passed away. There was much care discernible in these flowers, some possessing great bows, the like of which I had never seen before except for the occasional deceased royal or celebrity whose final rest, positively drowning in mountains of flowers, wreaths and bouquets, was broadcast on television or displayed in newspapers.

I decided to buy the two postcards from Éric, paying several euros for the pair and admiring them as I stood in the cosy shop. I began to read the back of one which had upon its aged card a beautiful series of sentences in extravagant handwriting. I could barely read it, but I noticed the address

to which the postcard was sent as it was Truchtersheim,
a little town just outside of Strasbourg where some of my
partner's relatives still lived. 'Do you like Goethe?' Éric
asked in methodically slow but understandable English. I
mentioned that I had recently developed an interest of sorts,
but that he was one of a number of people in Strasbourg's
history that I was now researching and curious about.
'Goethe,' Éric continued, 'is a dead man's writer.' He pulled
down his small, clear glasses to look at me as if to make sure
that I was not, in fact, a phantom myself before he made
his way back to his desk and continued with his studies.
I made to leave, but noticed a little box labelled '*Folklore
Alsacien*'. Most of the cards were brightly coloured: pictures
of flocks of white storks flying over the city, small girls with
blond pigtails and aprons doing things with flowers, men
chopping wood, and other seemingly twee things from the
lighter end of folklore. But one image stood out due to its
black-and-white nature in this multicoloured compendium.
It took a while to understand what the illustration actually
portrayed, the line of clouds blending with what appeared
to be a man riding a horse. There was an old, crooked tree
to the right, and on closer inspection what appeared to be
a large house in the background. I couldn't make the rest
of the image out at all, so I asked Éric. 'More Goethe?' he
asked, unusually. I was unsure what he meant. '*C'est le roi de
fées*, err chasing… in chase,' he said. I understood enough to
know that the white aspect of the illustration, taken on first
viewing as just a simple man on horseback, was actually the
Erlkönig, floating like a banshee after the rider who seemed
to be cradling a child, perhaps his son, from the seductions
of the creature. It was too prophetic to put back among the

other images in the box, so I turned to Éric and put a single euro on the table in exchange before heading back over the road to the flat. Taking the lift, I flicked through the pictures again and again, knowing that I would find myself staring from the window regularly in the direction of Éric's shop and its endless distractions from then on. I was glad to have found it, as if it was the key with which I could fully unlock the city, matching places in the present with images of the past. It was while admiring these postcards, now in the comfortable warmth of the flat with a small coffee brewing in the red cafetière in the kitchen and a cigarette lit, that I received a phone call from my partner who had, among other things, an unusual and timely request.

Monsieur Maurice was incredibly particular about his attire. It was said by many that, such was the care he took in the exact cut and quality of his clothing, his own work as a writer would frequently suffer if he could not consider his own view in the looking glass without total satisfaction with what he saw. He was a great admirer of early Strasbourg clothing culture from the days of strict rules about attire for both men and women. There was incredibly precise legislation regarding the design of men's clothes, with due attention paid to the length of certain capes, the qualities of material used to make such clothes, and even the number of particular adornments such as ribbons and other accessories. These items all denoted a complex system of class that was very important to the city in the days when it was a power in its own right; still using its own currency, making its own weapons and speaking its own variant of Alsatian. Monsieur Maurice was not to be argued with in regard to his clothing, even though his time was well beyond the days of such rules and regulations. His cape would flow down towards the floor and onto the cobbles as he walked with esoteric allure, exerting his own particular authority over the working class of Strasbourg simply through his demeanour. Some days, so it is recorded by an inquisitive neighbour and diarist, he would not leave his house on Rue Sainte-Hélène for, catching a glimpse of himself in the glass of his window, he was often seen to be earnestly alarmed and appalled, walking back into his house and not to be seen until the following day, or even for several days if particularly unsatisfied with the cut of his trousers or the collar of his shirt. Monsieur Maurice was also a noted eccentric and collector of strange items over which he became increasingly paranoid during the turbulent times in the city's history. Anything, as long as it was a distraction from his writing and the folly of ongoing politics.

One of Monsieur Maurice's most prized possessions at the time was the noted Zurich Cup: a golden chalice with multiple designs upon its metallic surface, a long thin stem and a small base that, surprisingly, managed to balance the large cup perfectly. The item was given to Strasbourg in the 1500s by the Swiss city in order to cement the relationship between the two. The trade between them was growing due to the Rhine, which several of Strasbourg's waters originally flowed within or towards, especially a canal known as the *Rheingiessen* which has since been filled in. The poet Johann Baptiste Fischart wrote about the cup with some grace and exuberance: 'Take us to Strasbourg, which adorns your banks, and in front of which you pass with pride.' Such words are engraved on a statue dedicated to the poet on Rue de Zurich, itself named after the trading relationship with the Swiss city as a trading tributary, down towards the end of this long road and beyond. Today, the statue's many details are largely hidden by moss, since its peculiar fountain-like design retains water whenever the weather is bad, allowing a new green skin to grow over the stone.

Monsieur Maurice would often invite people to pay homage to the cup when it was in his possession, allowing private visits to his house on a monthly basis, which in itself was an attraction of antiques. He would coax visitors into his grand living room, in the centre of which the Zurich Cup would be sat in theological splendour, as if it were a holy relic ordained by Christ. Chairs would be brought in so that admirers of the Zurich Cup could sit in comfort while they gazed at its designs, sometimes staring at their own reflection in the shining gold, their skin now rendered burnished and orange by the metal. Candles would give the room the warm air of a holy place and many often recommended the event to their acquaintances, especially wealthy ladies of the famous Strasbourg houses who saw Monsieur Maurice's eccentricities as a worthy and rewarding diversion. The city was still rebuilding itself after the trauma of the siege, which in 1870 had lasted for fifty-two devastating days. In the decades after, when Strasbourg was ceded back to Germany via the Treaty of Frankfurt, such rituals were seen as a welcome diversion from the underlying tensions still rumbling on the continent. Monsieur Maurice, however, would not live to see its later calamities. In the closing years of the nineteenth century, Monsieur Maurice's house gradually shut its doors to visitors. The old collector, increasingly stubborn and insular, ceased to take pleasure from showing off his wares, especially the Zurich Cup which, for several years, various museums and universities had pestered to take off his hands, not least because of its unique value and historic link to both Strasbourg and Zurich.

He was still seen wandering through the city streets on occasion, his coat meticulously cut to be exact in the way it swept after him when walking along what is now Grand'Rue in search of daily bread. One neighbour claimed that the eccentric had even taken to drinking out of the Zurich Cup itself, seen one afternoon through a window to be using the cup like a goblet, taking deep gulps of red wine like a medieval king or knight of the realm. Monsieur Maurice would eventually pass over, his heart giving way on a walk while, most appropriately, heading near Rue de Zurich. It was said that, with it being a Sunday, he was on his way to what is now the Reformed Church of St. Paul. However, Monsieur Maurice clearly spotted Rue de Zurich on his path and decided to amble down it, spotting the statue that celebrated with equal gaiety the impressions which adorned his most prized possession. It was after enjoying this road that Monsieur Maurice was seen to collapse, on the junction between Rue de Zurich and Quai des Bateliers, clutching at his heart before finally fading from Strasbourg, down to the Rhine and towards somewhere unspoken. The cup, like many of his items, was eventually put in the care of what would become the Musée Historique de la ville de Strasbourg, where it still stands on display. It was Monsieur Maurice's lips that touched the cup last, however; in honour of the forging of links and friendships between nations, cemented with gold and wine.

Truchtersheim, the small village in the countryside near Strasbourg where my partner's family mostly lived, lay to the north-west of the city, heading towards the mountains of the Parc Naturel Régional des Vosges du Nord which hang in the distance from almost any point when standing in the town. Though there is a feeling of the Old World that comes with the area's many outhouses and large, private faux-mansions, the town is relatively new in other ways, surrounded by a retail estate and a factory, and with even the oldest of buildings usually being modern refurbishments embellishing older designs. The houses are mostly terracotta, pink or various shades of traditional colours broken up by wooden beams typically found in the Alsatian departments. I had only been to the town a few times before with my partner, and so it was with some surprise that I found myself heading towards a bus depot, uncomfortably close to the train station with its hints towards the airport, with the intention of catching a bus to this town. My partner had rung to see that I was okay, his suspicions no doubt raised regarding my extended stay in his flat in Petite France over Christmas. 'Has something happened?' he had asked on the phone a few nights before, when he called after my wanderings in search of Goethe. I struggled to talk with him, his concern obviously false, music playing loudly in the background of wherever he was. 'Well, I hope you would tell me if there was anything wrong.' He continued in this interrogative manner for a few minutes longer before segueing into details regarding his trip, the comforts and discomforts of travel and how he missed his family. He failed to even question my Christmas plans. I managed to smuggle in details regarding how I would probably stay in Strasbourg for the winter, his voice giving the impression of shrugging off the suggestion as normal, only adding a further detail about how much he would need to cover the costs of using his amenities, and that it would be something to sort out on his return. The feeling of hatred rose up within and surprised me; that the man I had travelled so much to see was inducing what could only be described as rage, a feeling previously reserved only for those who had criticised my work publicly in papers and journal entries, or for my parents. The things I missed about him, his physical presence, was replaceable and really it was his room here that I warmed towards, even then mostly blank and devoid of character; my partner being someone who carried his personality with him. But he was a kind soul, as my mother had affectionately put it, knowing that it was equally an insult towards me. *Why couldn't you be so friendly and talkative like him, you don't deserve him, Isabelle.* I cringed slightly when telling him of my plans, not least because I phrased the statement as 'I would like *to winter* in Strasbourg, if that's okay?' recalling the dialogue of some aristocratic character from an old novel. In other words, I was staying in his flat until the seasons turned. The words filled my mouth with an awkward shape, as if I couldn't quite recall who I really was, and for the first time since I had found out about my father's death, I realised fully that I was fading slowly into an older time and entirely of my own volition.

The Erl-King, with his malevolent visitations, merely hastened this temporal travelling with his occasional nightly visits and violent pleasures. Commenting on how unusual I sounded, my partner suggested that I go and see some of his family, perhaps to break up the solitude that he assumed was engulfing me on a daily basis. I could not bring myself to tell him of my talks with Brice, Michel or Éric, or even my watching Farid as he conducted cars to empty spaces in the busy car park outside the flat. This was *my Strasbourg*, the world that I was fading into, and the sharing of this wintery world would have broken the swelling spell that was dragging me pleasurably under the damp pavements within tenderly vile embraces. 'You should visit *grand-maman* in Truchtersheim. I'm sure she would be happy for the company and she has so many stories to tell. She used to live near the Hôtel du Dragon on Rue du Dragon. We've probably walked past her when she was there and not even noticed. We're so blind together sometimes,' he laughed in a forced fashion. He would only ever criticise by insinuation. I agreed to go and visit *grand-maman*, not least because I felt that Goethe had not provided anywhere near enough of a world to immerse myself within and I needed to escape further from the kisses of bloodied lips, but also to bring to an end to this conversation. 'Oh, before you visit,' my partner said before hanging up to continue his travels, 'we used to call her the monster when we were younger after a story we were told because she's a little intimidating and rude in that old way, so don't be offended if she's a bit brisk with you. I know what you English are like.' He was gone in a click and I instantly began to search for *grand-maman*'s address and figure out the best route to get to the town, the panic setting in now I was on someone else's schedule, and someone possibly difficult at that. The old woman was to be forewarned of my visit later that evening by my partner before he caught the train to Lima or some such place – I didn't listen fully – and so I found myself wandering to the bus depot two days later without much memory of the intervening time in between; just pleasurable scratches upon my neck and thighs to accompany the growing maps on my arms.

The bus depot was on the other side of the Ill and uncomfortably outside of my territory of old Strasbourg. I felt the sense of discomfort rise as the amber hues of the town's old buildings changed to greyer layers of concrete and buildings in more modern styles that I associated with London. The depot sat behind the Place des Halles shopping mall, and my already chaotic journey was further waylaid by the security now protecting all entrances to the Christmas Market. Worrying that it would seem rude to turn up to someone's house at this time of year without some sort of gift, I stopped at one of the little wooden shacks put up in Petite France and bought the first thing I could see. It was a small packet of biscuits wrapped in a thin red bow. The biscuits were cut into the shape of a star and mostly brown but with one side of each star entirely covered in icing sugar. I later learned after this trip that such biscuits have folkloric resonances, being a German tradition at Christmas that stayed in Strasbourg after its transfer back to France, called the *Zimtsterne* or the Cinnamon Star biscuit. I'd buy bags of them after the Christmas period, their price reduced greatly after the season and their gritty, cinnamon taste addictive. The bus journey meandered through the countryside, mostly farmland which was rendered with a murky winter glow, cut through only by the morning hoarfrost that lay on the churned-up ground. It was a mostly flat plain, rather like Norfolk with its endless horizons. There were corridors of pylons that stretched for miles into the distance, even further than the mountain range on the horizon in fact, which began suddenly rather than with some warning of a slowly growing incline. I could not feel anything other than the bump of the occasional hole in the road as we passed through each small town that surrounded Strasbourg; Wolfisheim, Oberhausbergen, Mittelhausbergen, Niederhausbergen, Dingsheim and Wiwersheim before finally a quaint sign for Truchtersheim appeared. It was followed by several cut-out sheep, a strange wooden man sat on a log and a variety of small shops which led the way towards the centre of the residential town.

I knew my stop was after a small shop that, according to the online street view, retained a faded picture of Johnny Hallyday in the window, his incredibly tanned face now drained to a sun-dyed blue and white. Thankfully, the poster hadn't been changed since the street-view car had last driven through, alerting me that it was time to get off. The town was virtually empty of people apart from an old man so hunched over that it was a surprise to see him move off in the same position rather than stand up straight, having mistaken him for someone picking something up off the ground. I had said that I would arrive at *grand-maman*'s house before midday and hoped that my partner had told his grandmother that I would not be staying too long, worrying that the old woman may have prepared a meal. Her house was far into the residential streets near a water tower, the imposing building only a few minutes away from where the coach had left me near the town's small museum. Each road seemed even emptier than the last, as if the whole of the town had been constructed as a show home for a retail company. My mind wandered, considering how fitting some of the countryside that hid at the end of every street would be for Goethe's *Erlkönig* or my Erl-King. A small forest littered the horizon at the end of the view, with a dirt track that looked as if only carts had traversed it, rather than the many large cars that sat ominously outside each house, implying nothing less than the area's wealth. *Grand-maman*'s house, so I remember thinking, seemed genuinely older than the others that surrounded it but, I later considered, perhaps the foreknowledge of the age of its occupant had affected my perception.

I let a large metal knocker drop on the heavy wooden door, resembling several of the genuinely old doors of houses around the Ill in Strasbourg, especially on Quai Charles Frey where, in summer months, I had stopped several times to look at the detailed stone carvings that hang above many of them. No one seemed to be making their way towards this door so I let the knocker fall again, adding force to its movement which induced a loud bang and, even more surprisingly, the sound of an old woman's voice now quite close to the door exclaiming, *'J'arrive, j'arrive!'* The large door creaked open and a small, round woman stood behind it in amusing contrast. 'Isabelle, *c'est bien ça*?' she asked, and I confirmed, shaking her hand, kissing her on each cheek and using the usual terms of French greeting that I was used to performing mechanically for each new relative or friend I had been introduced to. I walked into the house, two cats standing to attention in order to observe the new intruder walking into their domain. The house was bursting with

interesting objects: old furniture and paintings on every
wall, an array of differing glass animals made by Lalique –
including a beautiful orange frog that was sat casually on top
of an electricity bill – piles of old magazines, especially old
television listings, shelves of leather-bound books ranging
from Zola to Balzac, and even a small collection LPs which
were, from a glance, comprised almost solely of German
Romantics. She led me through to a large, dark drawing
room, as if taking me into the centre of some great web. The
black cat to my right followed in curiosity while its ginger
cohort ran to safety up a flight of white wooden stairs,
equally littered with piles of objects lying in the shadow of
a grandfather clock. At first sight, the main room was just
as chaotic, but a strange sense of order began to form after
sitting in the room for several minutes, largely dictated by
an old roaring fireplace that was crackling and keeping
out the winter. Before I could begin to make small talk in
French, she had taken the biscuits that were hanging limp
in my hand, given a swift but brisk 'Merci!' and sat down
in a large leather chair by the fire, already some way into
unwrapping the small red ribbon from the top of the bag.
I slowly gathered myself together and made room on the
chair further from the fire, moving some small plates that
bore typically Alsatian designs of young men and women
underneath some dried food remains. I was beginning to
regret agreeing to this meeting with *grand-maman*, whose
name, it occurred to me then, I didn't even know. I had
never asked my partner and he had never mentioned her
actual name, only the detail of her old-fashioned nature and
being referred to as the monster when he was younger. I
panicked before the room distracted me from my worries,

taking in the surroundings while concluding that I would
do my utmost to avoid having to speak her name. *Grand-
maman* ate several of the biscuits vigorously, the sugar from
the little cinnamon stars seeming to give her a greater lease
of life, visibly brightening her persona with unusual speed.
She sat back for a moment, taking in the flavour and the
feeling of the biscuits before surprisingly starting to speak
in disjointed English.

'I'm never myself when hungry,' she said. 'I'm glad D.
arranged this visit as he mentioned you were all alone in
Strasbourg. Well, I'm alone here so,' she continued, 'we
should have lots to talk about.' Her more confident cat, which
I learned was called Georges, made himself comfortable in a
small gap between my leg and the chair. The action seemed
to open the old woman up further. Cats know who to trust,
I thought. We spoke in fragments but at length about my
stay in Strasbourg, my relationship with her grandson, my
impression of his parents, and my various interests in the
city. It was only when my eyes wandered that something
caught their attention. In the middle of telling *grand-maman*
of my pleasure in rummaging around the stalls at the
market on Rue du Vieux-Marché-aux-Poissons, I glanced
at a number of objects that sat upon the fireplace. There
were several photographs, a postcard and, most unusually,
a piece of amber which was the most beautiful I had ever
seen outside of a museum. The wall behind it glinted with
an orange hue but the stone itself shone with the reflective
qualities of a mirror. The conversation was beginning to die
down, especially because my mouth was dry from doing
most of the talking and I had yet to receive the offer of any
sort of drink. But *grand-maman* quickly spotted my curiosity

regarding the objects on the fireplace, turning to me with what can only be described as a mournful smile. 'That's the shelf,' she said, 'where I put my grandfather. I never met him properly, he went mad after the First World War but he still means a lot to me, so I keep him there. The fire warms the amber you know, and warm amber has great power for relaxing rooms.' I asked if I could look closer, knowing full well which object was of most interest. 'That,' I asked rhetorically, 'is Goethe, isn't it?' The postcard was an artist's portrait of the writer, one I had yet to see in my days of searching for images of the writer online, battered around the edges, stained with what looked to be coffee, and with a circular tear towards its topmost corner on the right.

I was most taken with Goethe's incredibly large hat, resembling a *kugelhopf* more than any sort of reasonable headwear. More importantly, I couldn't quite believe it; looking around expecting to find a fourth wall to break. But there was nothing, just the coincidence, the chance, or instead the agency of a higher, malevolent force. 'Oui,' *grand-maman* answered after a moment, 'that's Goethe. My grandfather liked his work. He wanted to be a writer before the war but never had the chance. The war started and he left his interest back in Strasbourg. But he carried that postcard with him until he was wounded and sent back to one of the hospitals near Lyon; I can't remember which.' I could not contain my excitement, blurting out that my own interest at that precise moment was in Goethe's life and work, having only mere days before walked to the statues of him in the university quarter, as well as visiting the road where he had lived before that. 'Well,' she said, 'you look the type to enjoy Goethe, I suppose.' I wasn't quite sure what this meant at first, recalling the words of the seller in the old postcard shop, but it became clearer as our conversation meandered on. 'My mother used to say,' she mumbled in between the crackling of the fire, 'that her father was always a followed man. Her own mother, my grandmother, had said the same, the pair having been together since childhood in Strasbourg. There was a sense, how can I describe this in English, that Édouard – his name was Édouard Roussel, I should have told you before – was *followed*, always looking, watching for something even as a child. He was a looking child, always looking,' she said. I started to connect this to her perception of me in that, clearly, she could see that I was myself being followed by something, the thoughts of my father perhaps, or worse.

I wondered whether she could see things behind me, or was aware of spirits circling the house in the empty streets outside waiting to take their pleasures from my body and soul. 'Édouard read Goethe from a young age, especially *Faust*. My grandmother told my mother that he became obsessed, when back from the war, with a *Faust* film simply because the image of the Devil overlooking the town looked similar to Strasbourg. He saw Goethe as a good luck charm of sorts which is why he carried that card with him. I know his fellow soldiers a found it very odd, carrying a postcard of a German writer. My mother said that he had admitted he often lied about who the postcard was of when asked about it. He even said it was Rousseau once, imagine!' she said laughing. The postcard would have fitted well with the others I had bought of the Goethe statue – since lined up along the skirting board in the living room of the flat – but knew that asking for it was out of the question. Instead, I asked to take a photo of the things on her memoriam shelf, and for her to tell me about Édouard, almost as a consolation for not being able to complete my collection. She agreed and, almost as if a password had been provided granting access to her friendly side, she immediately bobbed slowly towards her kitchen and made some herbal tea, a mixture of lavender and orange, which gave the room a further heady atmosphere as she brought a teapot with matching Alsatian designs in on a small tray. 'Well,' she continued, 'you must understand that all of this was a long time ago and that I was only a child and never properly met the man. I'm sure D. would be very surprised to find how interested you are in all of this! He's never been especially interested in history, always a practical boy. I can only repeat what my parents, and especially my mother, told me about her father as my memory is not quite there. You understand *évidemment*. Well, I remember,' she said, 'the first time I was told about *grand-père* Édouard was after he had died. My mother had caught me handling that piece of amber up there. Anything that I was told not to touch,' she made a swiping gesture with her hand that belied her great age, 'instantly became treasure and this really was treasure. To explain why not to touch it, aside from its value, my mother sat me down in our house, further down the road from here, and told of its meaning to her father. And you know, just like the Goethe postcard, the amber had been a lucky charm, so he had told my mother when young. He found it in the forest just over the hill apparently.' I was more intrigued how this old woman's grandfather had linked Goethe with the piece of amber than the actual history, but instead of explaining, *grand-maman* segued into further stories of Édouard, using the photographs on the mantelpiece. 'He joined the army very early. I think he wanted to get away from his father who was a brute apparently, a bully of the town; *le tigre de Truchtersheim*. Édouard had joined a regiment further south near Lyon and spent a good deal of time there, always accompanied by his piece of amber, his postcard of Goethe and some books. Like many young men at that time, he should have been a writer or at least an artist. He was apparently very talented and always in the middle of some book which never seemed to end. If only his father hadn't been such a bad man, he would have perhaps been less keen to join up,' she said. She showed me a blurry picture of a group of people outside a country house. Some were wearing military uniform and the others, probably their wives I thought, were stood in the middle while two children sat on the ground. The picture, though clearly sunny, seemed to have the quality of a snowstorm due to the blurriness, not unlike those showers of snow then descending upon Strasbourg.

'Édouard is on the right. That's the house further down the road, before most of the new buildings were added. We had unspoiled countryside here, you know.' I pictured Édouard carrying the Goethe postcard in his pocket, perhaps rubbing up against the piece of amber. 'It was a miracle he didn't lose either,' I said to *grand-maman*, but she merely shrugged and continued. 'It was a miracle he didn't lose his life. Anyway, he was shot at some point in some great battle where many men were killed, sent back from the conflict and spent the rest of the war recovering from the wound – I can't remember where.' I wasn't sure if she was discussing Édouard's place of rest or the position of his wound, but it mattered little either way. I still could not understand the connection and so asked about Goethe again. 'Perhaps,' I began, 'he continued his studies of Goethe when in his sickbed?' 'He believed the amber stone had saved his life and would talk obsessively about it protecting him. Quite mad. I remember my mother, however, would often say that she wasn't sure if he was talking about the bullet wound or some other danger she couldn't make him discuss. Since childhood he had developed an aversion to the forest over the way, reading too many stories; something my mother said once when I had nightmares about Hans Christian Andersen's stories. The wolf... oh *horrible*! He was always a horrible writer; I never read any to my children.' 'But,' I asked, 'was it Goethe or his writing that gave him nightmares?' It was pretty clear that it was something Goethe had written, and I had a strong suspicion as to which work he had read.

'*Faust* supposedly gave him nightmares for weeks. I only know this because my own mother had developed a sort of aura regarding the book because it was almost forbidden when she was young. She would say that Édouard would almost tease its contents out, saying that one day he would read it to her and her brother or, if they were misbehaving, use it almost as a threat. That wasn't really what *grand-père* Édouard was obsessed with, however.' '*Erlkönig*?' I asked swiftly, drawing her almost into a corner where she could no longer meander off-topic. '*Oui! Comment as-tu su?*' her formality slipping in surprise. I told her that I had been re-reading the poem in recent weeks, though I lied for it was merely days since I had last considered the writing and its chief character who had slowly developed corporeality in the streets of Strasbourg, especially at night; like a nightmare, shared by all and never resolved, dreaming of his touch and his brutal joys, given and taken. 'Well,' she said, 'that is a coincidence. Yes, he supposedly had nightmares for months after reading about the *Erlkönig* and became convinced that such a creature was haunting the forest nearby, where he would walk to get to his school in the other town over the way. I imagine that's why he was a followed child to his own mother and why my mother thought the same. You know,' and she laughed to herself when saying this, 'I think the postcard was more of a defence against this king of the – what's the English, fairies? – yes fairies, than against German bullets. To think of such a thing!' I went over to the mantelpiece and asked if I could handle the amber. *Grand-maman* surprisingly agreed. The stone was pristine and smooth, clearly worn down from being rubbed by both hand and pocket. Yet its colour still shone, and when held up to the eye it rendered the whole world with an orange shade, not unlike the streets of Strasbourg on sunny days when the rays reflected off the warmly painted buildings. Though now housed in a metal stand with three legs, I noticed a small hole in its upmost part, clearly where a piece of string or some such thing was wound through to turn it into a necklace of sorts. *Grand-maman* saw that I had seen this hole and commented, 'Yes, it's strange isn't it. *Grand-père* Édouard had said that he had liked to feel the stone near his heart and wore it often around his neck. The heart was what the *Erlkönig* went for when seeking to take his children, you see,' she said. I had visions of this creature, floating after the lone child in Truchtersheim's forests, waiting for the fatherless infant to falter in its journey, his hands reaching in through the ribs to take the prized heart. I couldn't help but share some sense of empathetic fear with the blurred man in the photo.

> *'Be calm, stay calm, my child;*
> *Through dry leaves the wind is sighing.'*

'*Grand-père* Édouard was awarded for his bravery and rose a few ranks after the war, though he had left the army by the time my mother was born, much to the dismay of his seniors. He was working various odd jobs but had trouble due to his injury, which still ached, apparently. It was around this time when his obsessions began again,' she said. 'He would roam around the area for hours, even at night. More houses were being built and the neighbourhood was gradually growing and becoming friendlier, so my mother used to say. But *grand-père* Édouard would disappear often. Jacqueline, my grandmother, was left to look after my mother while Édouard was becoming more unstable. My mother was incredibly embarrassed by this as a child, as the other children called him *Édouard le fou*.' I mentioned to *grand-maman* that, from what she had told me, Édouard sounded like he had some sort of early-onset dementia or perhaps what in his day would have been called shell shock, judging from his behaviour. 'I had noticed a similar behaviour with my own father before he hanged himself in Crystal Palace, a distance,' I said, 'always walking and never letting anyone know; disappearing for days until, after bothering the police, we'd end up finding him sat on Gipsy Hill looking out over the city; enjoying Zola's view, he used to say.' This was the first time I had mentioned my father or his action to anyone since his death and a silence filled the room, *grand-maman*

clearly perceiving a release on my part. She began talking
again with a clear goal to fill the void opening in the room
and avoid asking further about this suicide. I imagined her
questioning why her grandson had failed to mention such a
thing. 'Édouard once told my grandmother that he had found
that piece of amber in the woods over the way, though no one
could quite believe it. It was, he supposedly had said many
times, his secret treasure as a child, found one day when
scared and lost deep in the trees. Goethe would protect him in
later years, but it was the amber he had found in the ground
that he believed in when young.'

I thought about the likeness between the madness of
Roussel and my own, both hiding from spectres of lost
fathers, looking for treasure in the form of trinkets. In many
ways, Édouard's story chimed with my own feelings towards
the *Erlkönig*: that the creature was paternal of sorts, much
more than the father of the actual tale whose ignorance led
to his son's demise on the cart. His care was a morbid ruse,
a horrific reality. But the monstrous being was something to
grab hold of, filling the space left by my partner's absence.
There was even some crossover in the tale; that there was no
Erlkönig really, just a father's ignorance. It was his inability
to listen to his child's concerns, manifesting in the creature; a
form of coping mechanism for a parent unaware of their own
dereliction of duty. *Grand-maman* continued talking, though
I felt the weight of my father's deliverance passing from my
lips and the atmosphere slowly lifted in the room, in spite
of what the subject turned to. 'Édouard,' she said, 'became
more and more ill. My mother gave birth to me when he
was not all that old, but I don't remember him much at all.
He was quickly sent to an asylum, quite far away I recall,

perhaps Bonn near Cologne. That seems to be right. He must have convinced the doctors there that he was perfectly sane as I know he was back in Truchtersheim after only a year, wandering again around the town and quite cheery. He died, *évidemment*. Not too far from here, near that forest in fact, my mother told me. He had taken to wandering that field where the, err, what's the English?' – she made a triangle shape with both arms pointing upwards. 'The pylons?' I asked. 'Yes, with the wires, almost like the French then: *pylônes*. He would walk regularly where they are now and back around over the hill, though there weren't really any pylons there in those days, at least not that I can remember. Maybe there were. He was found holding his amber, though he didn't have the Goethe postcard on him. He had stopped carrying that long before, apparently. He was said to have had a heart attack over in the fields, though my mother once mentioned suicide. There was never any evidence of such a thing – what would D. think of me telling you all of our family's secrets! – but I know that, to my mother, his death was unnatural. She knew how scared he was of that forest, even as an adult, even after service in the war, even after treatment in Bonn... *Voilà.*' The fire crackled and I was glad to be indoors, not least as the winter air occasionally seeped through the gaps in the old window frame, highlighting the drop in temperature outside. The cat that sat upon my chair stretched its legs and, after a stroke of its shining fur, it meandered lazily off into another room. I began to make my excuses to leave but *grand-maman* wanted to know more about me and my stay in Strasbourg. Perhaps she wanted me to talk about my father, curious about the change audible in my voice when I had let slip about his death.

'I must go,' I said, 'but I've had a lovely afternoon and
thank you for the tea.' *Grand-maman* looked at me with a deep
stare, her eyes rendered warmly orange by the reflection of
the fire. 'You know,' she began, 'Édouard may have died
suddenly and did have a tragic life, but I think, and I may
be wrong,' she shrugged, 'I think he may have actually died
satisfied, if my mother is to be believed.' The word 'satisfied'
hung in the air and I wasn't quite sure what it meant, but it
had an effect upon my mind in that I felt deep down that I
had some clear feeling of grief. Had my father been the same,
seeing the end of the line with an out of character optimism?
The thought made me angry, so angry in fact that I forced
myself to gaze into the fire, as if its flames could burn the
rage from my mind. 'He missed Strasbourg,' she said finally,
'but don't we all sometimes?' I stood up and she followed, the
crumbs from the cinnamon stars falling onto the terracotta
tiles of the floor. I waved her a farewell from the bottom of
the path and made my way slowly through the town back to
the single steel post that indicated the bus stop. There was,
of course, no shelter or even any vague evidence that a bus
would stop there, so it required faith to remain. But, staring at
the horizon line, the urge grew within me to walk for a small
while and so, checking the time briefly on my phone, I let my
legs take me towards the forest. Maybe the *Erlkönig* – it *did*
sound better in German – would pay me a visit and drag me
into the woodland, to take me at will and thrust me into the
frozen earth. I could see my fingers scratching in pleasure at
the hard soil, filling the gaps under my fingernails with dirt
as terrible movements buried us both, deeper and deeper, my
body writhing in the mud. The road was wet, perhaps like
the day when Goethe left Strasbourg, the city finally fading

into the sky as his trailer headed for Frankfurt but forever retained within him like an insect caught in the sap of a tree. I could see the forest that Édouard obsessed over, the tops of the trees shuddering in the winter light. I didn't want to see any more trees – my father had ruined trees – so I walked to the pylon corridor, past a small industrial estate where the cut-out sheep stood surreally on the embankment. There was only the road and pavement then, surprisingly busy with traffic that sped by with great jets of noise and air. There was also a wide path, probably designed for cyclists, though I failed to see any that day. The wires of the pylons extended far towards the mountains in one direction and into the flat land on the other, large bales of hay sometimes piled high like the early building blocks of a great cathedral or church.

The bus back would be a welcome journey, to Strasbourg and my island. The vehicle meandered through the small towns, filled with street corners threatening to reveal a dark shroud or fragment of gliding cloak, but never quite allowing it. It would have been too overt, too open for the Erl-King to show himself in such a scenario. He couldn't have used me then, in such a public place. I imagined nights again, nights of his terrible visits to my room, wondering if his pleasures and the hanging corpse of my father would ever truly *leave*. Goethe's contested last words came to mind – '*Mehr licht!*' – and I wondered then if the light he required as he slipped into darkness was not of some transcendent white glow as in clichéd representations of death, but instead of an orange hue, like that found on the streets of a city from his past, now seen through the amber stone of a last memory or a forgotten love.

2

Monsieur Moreau was a noted family man. He lived with his siblings, his wife and his children in a large house near Place Broglie, and the locals often noted their group walks. Such a group was easily recognisable for there was always the pairing of the Moreau sisters – Josette and Liliane – Monsieur Moreau's two sons – Félix and Raoul – and, of course, Madame Moreau, who was a noted socialite in various Strasbourg circles in her younger years. The family were also noted for their patriotism, at least of the kind proudly espoused by the patriarch, who had several stories that were repeatedly told to the two young boys so that, in later years, they would hopefully grow up with the same fine principles and beliefs. Monsieur Moreau, when walking with his young sons alone, would often take them to the centre of town in order to tell them the same story. The mayor of the town in years gone by was a man called Philippe-Frédéric de Dietrich, who lived at 17 Rue des Charpentiers. It was at his house where, so it is said, 'La Marseillaise' was first sung as a patriotic act, rendered by an unknown singer while accompanied on a harpsichord. Such an event is known, even today, due to a letter sent to Basel from the mayor's wife to her brother, who recounted the event in minor detail. Some still suggest that it was Strasbourg's mayor himself who had sung on that occasion, though it was not to be verified for he was eventually murdered at the hands of Robespierre during the Reign of Terror. 'This,' Monsieur Moreau would say to Félix and Raoul, 'is the house where our great anthem was first sung.'

One of his sons would keep an extensive diary, edited into a memoir in later years, as he refused to discuss his father in the public realm for most of his adult life. Monsieur Moreau was very proud that he lived within walking distance of where this patriotic emblem of France was supposedly born. Moreau was, according to the diary of Madame Moreau, not a particular competent father, and he was lucky to have three pairs of women's hands besides his own to keep the boys in check. For Félix and Raoul were renowned for mischief in the central district and were often at the heart of various elaborate pranks for which their father, when eventually finding out about such affairs, would beat them severely. On one occasion, Félix Moreau was so badly beaten, after a mishap regarding the market near Place Kléber, that he was hospitalised and spent the remainder of his childhood with a minor limp which he was terribly bullied about, even at university.

Monsieur Moreau considered it his moral duty to mete out such punishments. It was arguably the only aspect of parenting that he partook in, alongside his patriotic jaunts around Strasbourg. He had several regular haunts which he would drag his young sons to, even sometimes forcing them to avoid schooling, which they both loved thanks to the home tutoring by their aunts Josette and Liliane; the former a noted ceramic painter with an interest in history, and the latter a successful (though private) ornithologist who had great knowledge regarding the natural sciences. Monsieur Moreau would take the boys to the mausoleum at the Chancel of Saint-Thomas. It was here, after a brief stay at the Temple Neuf in 1751, where the remains of the Marshal of Saxony found their eventual resting place. Maurice de

Saxe was the illegitimate son of August II, King of Poland, and worked hard to overcome the difficulties of being a bastard child. He joined the German segment of the Army of the Holy Roman Empire at an incredibly young age, eventually to find himself the Marshal General of France. It was suggested by Monsieur Moreau that the figure owed some of his success to his estrangement from his father, forcing him towards independent thought and action in great haste far before his years. Monsieur Moreau had learnt about this history and often excused his dereliction of duties towards his own sons by proclaiming they would never be great men if he pampered them. 'They can be no Maurice de Saxe if I mother them like you do!' he once said to his wife, again recorded in her own private diary, kept in the secret compartment of a teak box adorned with designs portraying several orchids. Out of all of the rituals that he forced his sons to bear constant witness to and consider, the most important was visiting a painting of Louis XIV by Adam-François van der Meulen. It is not certain where the painting was housed at this point, but Monsieur Moreau seems to have been allowed access to it. He was certain that it represented all that was great about France and, most of all, never failed to point out that Strasbourg's cathedral could be seen in its lower left-hand corner. 'This was the place of great men, the true heart of France,' he once said to his sister in a debate regarding the wars, unaware of the irony of his statement.

Monsieur Moreau would eventually leave this world in disgrace after the death of his son Raoul. It is said that in a fit of rage induced by something Raoul had said, Monsieur Moreau had beaten him to death with the poker from a

fireplace set. Happening in front of several witnesses, including both of his sisters, Monsieur Moreau had little chance of escaping the French justice he so often admired. Monsieur Moreau was sentenced to death and executed promptly after the incident, Félix being left to be brought up by his two aunts and mother, though the latter was often too distraught for anything after the incident and became reclusive to the point of madness following the scandal. Félix grew up to read law at the University of Strasbourg, before following in the footsteps of Goethe and becoming a practising lawyer; not a writer of prose, however. Though he himself lived through the many calamities that soon befell the town, he lived until his mid-sixties, watching as his remaining family died one by one. The lone child never had children, such was his worry of somehow having inherited his father's quick temper. Félix was said to be greatly distraught as old age caught up with him, as he claimed to see his father's likeness in his own features. Such aspects came to haunt him in his dying days, the man often refusing to acknowledge that he had even known his own father when young or that he had had a brother. The man and the boy were forever connected by the violent action. In his final testament, Félix continued this denial until his dying day, suggesting days before he passed away:

'I had a mother three times over. But I did not have a father.'

What was to be gained from my self-imposed exile in Strasbourg? It had been several months since my father's death. He had – so I assumed from skim-reading the handful of messages sent by my mother in her confused states of seething hatred and incandescent sadness – been cremated and scattered somewhere. She still could not help herself in occasionally sending some vitriolic comment, however. I imagined he had directed that his ashes should be scattered somewhere in London: he was a London painter and had often gone on about the so-called London School, which he naively hoped one day to be remembered as part of. I had thought variously of my father, our haphazard relationship, the volatile home with my mother. I missed very little of it, but grief did not allow reality to fully display itself. Instead, a minority of happy memories kept reasserting themselves as if I was psychologically rewriting my history, my own tracts of unhappiness. Happy Christmas days were prominent, the occasional birthday when nothing was let down by either of them, a handful of budget holidays, all lovely. I thought of his disintegrating mind, never properly diagnosed; he had gone before his body had caught up. Really then, I had little to worry about in returning, and I certainly wasn't staying in the city waiting like a lost woman for the return of her partner from afar. In other words, I was now taking refuge in the city for no reason that was readily apparent to me. My responsibilities had been laid to rest, an email from the university had already demoted my new position and threatened to remove me entirely from the department subject to an official investigation if I failed to return for the upcoming semester. This was research leave, I had said, lying about funding body support for monographs on the city, all lies. I thought of potential money from some undisclosed will as a possibility of support if I arrived back jobless, but my mind was far from functioning or considering the practical aspects of living. *You always were irresponsible, Isabelle, privileged.*

The stories I had heard so far had developed addictive qualities at any rate, besides academic use, and I was feasting upon them, like the Erl-King upon my body, now thinner than it had ever been and criss-crossed with fleshy maps of scarred lines. I was walking specifically in search of stories rather than allowing them to happen by accident. The element of chance, on my part at least, had disappeared, and I was often left in my partner's dusty flat alone, craving things that could not be forced or reading old journal articles about minor aspects of the city's history; or simply waiting for that increasingly infrequent night when the Erl-King would visit and devour me before slipping away into the darkness. He seemed less and less inclined the more I took enjoyment from his violence. Luckily, Strasbourg was like a patchwork quilt, constantly revealing new designs, aspects, fabrics, colours, textures and ideas at every turn, and so I only needed a brief drift through its centre before someone would soon appear, brooding with great desperation to tell their story. They would slash their eyes, if only to be released of the burden of such stories. I had taken to frequenting various coffee shops once more with printouts of journal entries to read, waiting for people to talk. I walked an almost full circle of the centre, stopping intermittently between venues and drinking various milky mixtures of coffee and cream. I was back in the very centre, haunting the area around the cathedral and by the house, the oldest house in Strasbourg in fact, whose windows were made from the sliced rears of many hundreds of bottles of wine. I stared at Gutenberg's alias and he stared back at me, wandering down to the river past the sign indicating Jean-Hans Arp's place of birth and Goethe's room, the latter reminding me of *grand-maman* and the sad fate of her own grandfather. I had yet to properly consider Jean-Hans Arp, other than the unusual grouping of three important figures in such a confined space. I was soon to fall into another coincidence, leading to the city's history being further sketched in front of me, or perhaps, in hindsight, tricking me. I felt as if I were now a walking map of the city's generalities, joking to myself that I would make a reasonable tour guide for the centre if my French improved, though a guide plagued by spectres at the corner of their eye and probably not the most enjoyable company.

The road seemed bigger, as I had often walked it when the curios fair was on or the recently concluded Christmas Market, stalls such as Brice's framing new walkways which were smaller than the reality of the pavements. I stood still looking up at Jean-Hans Arp's plaque on Rue du Vieux-Marché-aux-Poissons, noticing how bland and formal it seemed for such an experimental artist and writer, before wandering home once more and daydreaming about when a ghost would appear in some venue or other to tell his story, of his life and work about which I knew next to nothing, except his role as part of the Dada movement in the early years of the twentieth century. I searched half-heartedly for images of his work online, noticing the strange shapes and forms that his collage and sculptural work took, before noting that he was a writer and poet too. This was something I had not known before researching him, only associating his name with the general image of Dada; appropriately, an ambiguous collage of faded materials. I was surprised not to have known this, another search revealing very little in the way of English translations of the artist's work. It was as if he was kept a secret on the continent, still bright and vivid from having been retained in storage, failing to pale in the constant light of British attention like so many other artists had. Even from finding pictures of the man online, of which there were few, with his short, slicked-back hair almost flat upon his head, a strange aura was perceivable. His story would, so I thought, come close to completing *something*. Mourning through the melted amber of the city's past, its history was soon to be rendered as an academic treatise through my research.

It was some days later, when I was again in the vicinity of Arp's plaque, when a person ready to help my research happily appeared. The rights to Arp's work had been guarded by his estate resulting in its lack of availability in translation, so I felt I needed someone to discuss him with more than I had with Gutenberg or Goethe. I searched that evening for volumes online and could find very little in English except for a single edition that was being sold for an astonishing amount of money. I knew then that I would have to try and read more French if I was to experience his work, and so I endeavoured to find a volume of his poems the following day in one of the city's bookshops. I could have ventured to any number of small bookshops that sat in the heart of Strasbourg, but opted for one on Grand'Rue which had multitudes of interesting things in its large window: new editions of Michel Foucault; multicoloured children's books, most of which followed cats going on adventures; photo books of the pictures of Raymond Depardon; and, as Christmas had only recently passed, some still-arranged decorations, messy tinsel and baubles which sat in garishly odd contrast to the volumes of books, printed by Folio, Gallimard, and *Les Éditions de Minuit* with their snow-white covers and simple blue-lined borders. I started to search the larger French Writers section, looking for Arp. A whole shelf was full of his poetry, housed alongside literature rather than in some other dedicated section. *Your father hates poetry, why did you buy him that?* I picked each volume up, noticing the beautiful texture of the paper used for many of their covers; as if the book had just been printed in the back room of the shop and left out like freshly baked bread. I knew that reading would be a struggle, especially poetry, as my ability to speak French had plateaued since my partner had gone on his travels. He took my voice away with him, I thought spitefully as I realised we hadn't messaged for a number of days and neither of us had barely noticed. I opted for the slimmest and cheapest volume I could find in the shop, accepting that my curiosity did not stretch far enough at that point to commit to the huge volume of collected works, interspersed with pictures of many of Arp's sculptures, not least for the reason that it weighed a great deal and cost roughly the equivalent of three weeks' worth of food and drink. My volume was called *La Grande Fête sans fin* or *The Great Endless Festival* or *The Great Festival Without End*. I could not decide on an appropriate translation, chiefly as I couldn't decide which sounded more poetic. The woman behind the counter greeted me with a friendly '*Bonjour*', placing a small sticker over the price on the book's cover and then wrapping it neatly in a small paper bag. I had only seen such care taken with food; her actions were not unlike those of a passionate fruit seller, tenderly handling delicate items that bruised easily.

The January rain was falling once more as I left the shop, standing in its small doorway to consider my options of where to go as water poured down. The cobbles of Grand'Rue were shining, and everyone was marching by at a quick pace, sometimes breaking into a run when their threshold for being soaked through was surpassed. I opted to walk quickly in the rain towards Place Gutenberg, crossing the tramlines on Rue de la Division Leclerc and through to the square where Gutenberg's shadow-self stood overlooking the wandering people. I wanted to cross the boundary of Arp's house once again with a sense of ritual caused by carrying the book; as if, like one of Gutenberg's mirrors, it would gain something from being in close proximity to the writer's birthplace, before stopping to read it. Once more I walked down Rue du Vieux-Marché-aux-Poissons to see his house and gather any radiant light from its walls, though the weather somewhat spoiled this offering. I must have paused abruptly on the pavement as a young couple in their teens almost stumbled into me: '*Désolé, pardon.*' They looked to where my eyes were wandering, but could see only the fashion boutique which sat beneath the plaque, water running down its glass windows. I imagined it was raining when my father had died; it was always raining in Crystal Palace in autumn. I had thought of him very little in the intervening weeks, perhaps putting my barrier up higher than it had previously been in order to avoid Christmas and the memories it would summon. The Erl-King had mostly vanished and lessened his visits at night, leaving me feeling frustrated and craving touch again. I was totally alone but that was for the best. I had lived in icy solitude, finally admitting such solitude in the weeks before to my partner. I was surprised my mother hadn't contacted him to plead for his help in bringing me back; that was the sort of game she liked to play, portraying herself as a caring mother, the victim in all of this. *It's a paint set, Isabelle, so you can grow up to be just like your father.* I soon left my daydreams and noticed that, for some time, I had been standing totally still in the rain, staring up at the building.

It was an unusually old building, seemingly containing three columns with the central column protruding outwards. There were three equal arches underneath on the ground floor where the boutique was housed, while the frames of each window looked to be made of very old stone; like the stones of graves I had seen in Kensal Green Cemetery once when looking for the grave of a writer I had admired as a teenager. Most unusual was the bust that sat underneath Arp's plaque. The head of a strange, demon-like creature leered out, a head that would have seemed mischievous, with its long snaking tongue sticking out, if not for its eyes which were unnervingly blank. It hinted at a disjoint in character; the maniacal nature of mischief and the cold, dead stare of malevolence. It shared that in common with the Erl-King; I imagined their faces were equally blank, absent. It made me want to walk on to avoid its glare and so I did, heading towards the river in search of refuge from the rain which had now soaked my coat right through and was slowly dampening the sleeves of my jumper. Even by my own hardy standards, I knew I was now unfeasibly soaked to the bone, and so quickly sought the nearest cafe. Unfortunately, this cafe happened to be a newly-built American chain, its garish sign so overt against the backdrop of the aged building it occupied that it seemed to make the area quiver with an unnameable temporal instability.

On sunnier days, I had seen the cafe draw looks of
dismay from passers-by, and it was only ever occupied
outside by the louder variety of tourists. But, at the time, it
was my only option, and so, rather than walking further to
find one of my usual cafe haunts, I stepped inside and did
my best to hide my disdain for its droning music, its clean-
cut seats and its questionable drinks. The heavy sound of
water hitting the windows told of a wise decision, and so
after ordering a drink, giving my first name to be written
on the cardboard cup and called out once ready, I headed
upstairs and sat down dripping on a cheap wooden chair.
What would Arp have thought of this surreal place? Its
designs were smooth and flowing, much like his sculptures
though there was rebellion in his simplifications. He'd have
probably liked it in a perverse sort of way. I put the damp
package containing the volume of *La Grande Fête sans fin* on
the table and opened the lid of the coffee. The edges of Arp's
book were darkened by water, so I made to dry it with one
of the napkins. Before opening it, I contemplated the cover,
admiring the red mountain adorning it. I recognised the
mountain, or at least I thought so at the time, noticing its
stark resemblance to a mountain I had seen on a trip to a
town in the south of Switzerland on the Italian border.

I began to make my way slowly through the poems,
falling into strange dreams, perhaps in an effort to avoid the
fact that my French was simply not good enough to tread
confidently through the words, instead latching onto specific
phrases and even designs that the words had crafted, rather
than taking in the overall meaning. I could feel the furrow of
my brow growing heavy and did my best to hide it from the
other customers of the cafe; a pair of young girls – probably

tourists, judging from their backpacks parked on the table – a woman and her dog whom I thought I recognised, and an old man who, when not staring down religiously at his newspaper, would apply a steady gaze at my volume of Arp, a gaze only broken each time by my own eyes meeting his, inducing their sharp return back down to the words crawling below him. His stare came to follow me to such a degree that I eventually had to put the volume of Arp down on the table and make do with idly daydreaming at the cheap print of coffee beans on the wall, blown-up to such proportions that it looked like a brown, desolate landscape. As soon as I had put the book down, the man stood up. He rolled his newspaper under his arm and made his way towards my table. His clothing seemed a much older style than most of the people I had seen walking the road, even on the day of the fair which drew a noticeably older and more eccentric clientele. His suit was baggy, made of grey tweed and he wore a beige mac which had been turned a darker shade by the rain outside, now only half dried. I could not tell whether he was attempting to grow a beard or was simply in need of a shave, though he later confessed, once we got talking, that his work as an academic had rendered all attempts at appearing a normal, fully functioning human being useless.

He stood above the table and asked very simply, '*Aimez-vous le travail de Arp?*' I took a minute to consider my answer as the tone was almost threatening, so I simply replied, '*Oui*,' in a stifled English way, hopefully alerting him that my French was going to be poor. My English '*Oui*' had the effect I desired as he instantly softened in tone and, without being invited, made a show of sitting down in the chair opposite

me, ruffling my carefully arranged table with his soggy
paper and a brown hat which he had somehow concealed
up until the moment it almost knocked my cardboard cup
of coffee over. 'So,' he said with a thick French accent,
'you are English and you're reading Jean-Hans Arp? What
a coincidence!' I confessed almost instantly, as if under
strict interrogation by some governmental force, that I was
trying and failing to read the volume of Arp as so little of
it was available in English. His laugh rang out through the
coffee shop and I felt a faint embarrassment at its volume,
physically shrinking into my seat. Every part of my body
language suggested that I did not know this man particularly
well. 'So,' he began again – a habit I eventually learned he
was entrenched in from our long conversation – 'you like
Jean-Hans Arp? His writing, his sculptures, *the genius?* That
volume is passable, passable; you should have bought the
full works, get the *gesamtkunstwerk* as some would say,
not that I would agree.' He laughed again, loudly, and I
confessed that I had looked at the volume in question but
could not afford it. 'I walked past his house before though,'
I said, trying to stem his laughter and guide him back to
the conversation. 'So, you should know,' he said, 'that by
your luck in coming here today, you can learn all about Arp.'
He emphasised 'Arp', holding back from slipping into '*moi*'.
'You know, you are very lucky, yes, that my job is actually to
write about Jean-Hans Arp, well Dada.'

I wasn't sure whether to believe him until he introduced
himself fully as Dr Patrice Ricard of Strasbourg University's
humanities department, 'with a specialism branching into
the *les arts plastiques*,' he added, as if his avoidance of this
detail was somehow my mistake. I couldn't quite believe it

and felt, as with many I had met and seen in the city, that this was absurd. I had thought the same when I first met Brice and had been proved wrong, though Brice had felt natural in the way he spoke and how history was simply a part of his life; I had not been looking for connections to Gutenberg. Here, I had been looking for a connection to Arp and Strasbourg had suspiciously provided it. 'So,' he began again, 'you want to know about Arp? I know better than most,' he said, 'and you know why? I'll tell you, yes? I had *connections* to Monsieur Arp, not personally of course – I'm not that old' – he laughed loudly again – 'but my family knew him. So, it's why I learned all about him,' he said, 'for my great uncle's sake.' I was already exhausted from this introduction, but I agreed to stay and listen, conscious that I had asked for this from the city and its spirit had somehow provided it.

I was indeed interested, but also worried at not taking in everything the theatrical academic would say, similar to the fatigue I'd felt at certain conferences where the information came in such quantity and at such speed as to render everything after the first hour a complete mystery. I got up and went to get another coffee before Dr Patrice interrupted. 'The English, always very kind, well, until recently yes? Ha! So, *un grand cappuccino, s'il vous plait*. Very good for your French practice,' he said loudly across the cafe, his words shooting over the heads of several other customers. I came back up the stairs with two large coffees, unusually nervous, almost not believing my own senses. 'So, did you know, apart from his local connection, that Arp had visions?' he said. 'Great visions. Have you been to Le Musée d'Art Moderne yet? Seen his work? No, well the internet is fine for now but still, you must go, this week in fact.' I told him of my own background, if only to cut him off, simply so he could edit his story accordingly before he completely exhausted me with friendly condescension. But, before he could go on, he stood up again.

'If you *really* want to know about Arp I will need some things. So, are you busy?' he asked. I said no, but professed wanting to avoid the rain, hoping with all my heart he wasn't going to invite me back to his office; that awful coded question older academics threw out like a disguised weapon. 'Well, that's no problem at all! I only need to collect some things to show you, I doubt you doubting English would believe half of the things I said without *evidence*.' I begged to differ but allowed him to continue, thankful I didn't need to go with him. He left in haste, this strange man, leaving the drink that I had just bought him and his newspaper, saying he would be back in a mere twenty minutes as his flat was only further down the river. 'Inherited from my great uncle who knew Arp!' he added as he slipped down the stairs into the rain. I sat drinking my coffee alone, idly trying to translate the poems of Arp again and wondering what Patrice was going to bring back. Arp had seemed troubled in the photos I had seen of him, his hair cut short like a prisoner's, his eyes darkened as his whole head looked downwards as if having just received the news of some great calamity. After some minutes of breaking the words down, one poem, *'La Plaine'*, clearly opened with the lines: 'I was alone with a chair on a plain, Which lost itself in an empty horizon.' It felt apt for my situation at that time; waiting for a man I didn't know to tell me things I perhaps wouldn't believe and show me things that possibly didn't exist. I struggled on with the translation, noting how the poem began to remind me of my father and his hanging body, which had been far from my mind for what had seemed an eternity; the eternity of Strasbourg. 'Time was only an abstruse ghost since nothing happened or changed,' wrote Arp.

The images were too strong, even with my feeble translation, and so I closed the book swiftly and slid it along the table as if it were a plate of food that had caused distaste. There was something off about the day, and I could swear that the people wandering by in the rain outside were in fact floating by the window, with movements like that of the Erl-King, wearing attire from another epoch. My eyes began to ache as if slowly blinded by strain, before the sight of my own reflection in the glass caused me to snap out of my state. My father was in the ground, like Arp, only Arp was more interesting. He had at least made a success out of his work and was not the failed painter of Crystal Palace. I grew impatient with Patrice, as it was clear these thoughts would continually invade if I didn't have some meaningful distraction soon. The damp volume lying limp on the table was certainly not working, its French causing me to drift in thought. It was just at the moment when I had begun to pack the book back into its paper wrapping that I noticed the eccentric academic bound past on the street below and into the coffee shop once more, dripping water as he walked quickly up the stairs. I was actually relieved to see him, at least until he began his sentence once more. 'So,' he said, 'I wasn't long, was I? Here, I've got what I wanted. Have another coffee and I'll tell you of Arp.' He let a folder fall to the table with a dramatic slap, making the older lady still sat at the table across the way jump, her little dog barking before she consoled it with kind words and fixed the back of Patrice's head with a cold stare; not that he noticed, being too engrossed in whatever it was he had brought. I still had half a bitter coffee, albeit lukewarm, and so assumed that he wanted another now that the previous one was positively cool.

I am, so I thought, very clearly not in England, as the person would have drunk the cold coffee gratefully with a pleasant smile rather than say what they really felt. It was something my partner found alien, often frustrating in fact, anger rising from my unhappy silence at his words, his actions, his choices. Honesty was expensive but it was the sort of refreshing mentality that was partly the reason why I had stayed in the city, why I had made the effort to come here more than my partner had to come to London. 'Gloomy city,' he had said one day while we were sat in Brixton. 'No one feels anything,' he had continued. Such a repression was impossible for him, yet he was not an extrovert, just simply and naturally free to feel and express. Everything was expressed here in Strasbourg but, ironically, it made for a great mask to cover the face of a very particular truth I was hiding from: that my father, no matter how much I hated him, no matter how much I had hated the household he had built with my harridan mother, had meant something to me once. Death had slowly drained the bile of my hatred and left only a shining jewel of fondness at the basin of my contempt. But I was about to hear the story of Jean-Hans Arp and that mattered more to me then, I thought, than the landscape paintings of a failed Crystal Palace *artisan*.

Patrice's folder had an address written on it in blue ink. I assumed it was his address as it read Quai des Bateliers, which was the road that ran along the other side of the river, and it seemed a reasonable distance for his recently undertaken run in the rain. There were some stamps in the corner which seemed quite old and had been printed over with the appropriate postal mark. But most important was that on the other side of the envelope was written 'Arp: *archives de premier niveau*', in a scrawled handwriting that hid the haggardness of the words. 'So, this is the initial archive of material that started my work on Arp,' Patrice said. He was surprisingly calm, despite now sipping what was easily his third or perhaps fourth coffee. It was as if he had changed character, from eccentric to tutor in the merest sleight of hand. He began to empty the contents of the folder onto the table in front of us, manoeuvring them with a delicacy that displayed the great value they clearly held to him and certainly belied their ordinary folder. There were a handful of photographs and postcards, but also a small brown book that was extremely thin and what looked to be some sort of sculpting knife with an unusual fragment embedded into its handle. 'This,' he continued, 'is the first collection of objects that began my research into Arp unofficially, before my work on Dada that led to actually studying the man as well as Sophie Taeuber-Arp, the artist and his partner. Most were given to me by my Great Uncle Claude, the man who knew Arp right up until he left for greater things,' he said. 'Claude was born here too and first met Jean Arp when he was, in fact, not Jean Arp but Hans Arp. After the war, the French authorities encouraged the name to be changed, but there was more to it than that. Hans was born at 52 Rue du Vieux-Marché-aux-Poissons, the road where we are now, in fact,' he added, gesturing out of the window, though the building with the plaque could not be seen from the angle of the window. 'They would meet regularly, my uncle and he, and they would exchange ideas for they both wanted to follow their creative passions which, at that time, leaned towards poetry. They studied together, debating the possibilities of language that had been opened up by Baudelaire, whom Claude adored, and Rimbaud, whom Arp adored. You know them of course? The English don't always know these people. Hans and Claude would meet regularly with a group of fellow students at a terrace on Place des Tripiers just over there, where they would debate regularly.'

Allowing him a pause I began to pick up some of the photos, assuming that the man in one of them was Claude. I was proven correct for Patrice instantly curved the photo down and pointed as I started to photograph them in detail on my phone. 'That's Claude with the woman who would become his wife, Anita, a German who moved here from Offenburg,' Patrice added, before letting me look at the photograph undisturbed. He made no effort to stop me taking pictures of them, perhaps able to see the researcher's gaze in my aiming for their perfect capture. I told him that I was in the midst of research, though lied about the current research project with much rigour as if I was talking to the head of my own department. The pair in the photograph were well dressed, I thought, and stood by a small lake. Claude's ears stuck out from his hat, but it suited him. They possessed the casual air of people working in creative circles; those that, through their own sense of detachment from the rigours of day-to-day life, can endlessly bend backwards or forwards and not snap or give in. 'So, that picture,' Patrice began again, 'is around the time that Arp had left Strasbourg but when they were still keeping in touch by letter. Look at my uncle's tie; it's marvellous, isn't it?' he suggested. I concurred, though I was more interested in the picture's surroundings as I seemed to recognise the style of the fence they were stood next to from somewhere.

I asked Patrice where it was, and he pulled out some of the photos from underneath the brown booklet. 'That's Parc de l'Orangerie, have you not been there?' I lied and said no, but had been there with my partner and had actually looked up the park's history when initially looking for it on a map in the summer of the previous year. I had even looked the park up in recent weeks, especially when in the depths of my obsessions as it was near Rue Herder. I recalled that summer's walk, following the Ill tributary all the way along to where it grew greener and the houses and shops thinned as the buildings increased in size. All of sudden the river turned, and a huge group of parliamentary buildings were there looking out over the river, huge cathedrals of glass that, in the clear summer's day of the walk, glittered with the infinite rays reflecting off them. I remember seeing a man made of stone behind the Council of Europe's building, protestors outside the Court of Human Rights who had made a makeshift riverside village of tents, and further protests outside the park itself. We were walking to meet a cousin of my partner who worked for the European Council, and the park was to be our meeting place.

We had waited on the great white steps of the building in full sunlight before she arrived and walked us into the park. 'The protestors have been causing trouble,' she had told us. A statue of the former French Prime Minister, Pierre Eugène Jean Pflimlin, had been vandalised and almost torn down by the protestors in the previous week due to their pleas

about the treatment of Turkish journalists seemingly going
unheard. The statue, at the time of walking, was surrounded
by veils of security tape with the bronze politician leaning
forward as if he was about to stride into the earth itself, but
this did not distract from the beauty of the park. There is
some debate about who built it, but the likelihood is that it
was probably originally designed by Louis XIV's gardener,
André Le Nôtre, later and ironically acquiring the orange
groves that gave it its name from a private estate during the
revolution. *You'll never visit his grave, I bet.* However, there
were now only a handful of the orange trees remaining,
kept pristine in a special greenhouse within the park as if
they themselves were now a museum piece. We had sat
eating lunch and talking on the grass, the clapping sound
of the white storks, who made their yearly nests on the
flat tops of the trees which avenue the park's pathways,
echoing through the air. I remember the park as a happy
place, an occasional stork gliding in to land; more confident
than the other birds in the area, with something knowing
in its movement suggesting that its position as the region's
symbol was known by the animal itself.

Patrice continued looking at the picture of Great Uncle
Claude. 'He was sad,' Patrice said, 'to hear of Arp's plans
to move to Paris, but knew it would be for the best. So,
they endeavoured to keep in touch by letter and it was not
long before Arp had sent his first letter to Claude's new
apartment, which lay on Quai des Bateliers overlooking the
river, the flat I actually inherited from him after his death.' I
could not help but notice the wry smile he gave me, unable
to hide the happiness that this acquisition had clearly
brought him. Academics coming upon such luck can never

quite believe it, in my experience. 'Claude,' he began, 'never actually opened the mail Arp had sent in the apartment, however, even with the balcony overlooking the water being one of the most beautiful spots in the town. He had on every occasion, he once told me, read such mail at the terraced cafe on Place des Tripiers, right over there. It was a sort of ritual he had. Arp's first letter to him contained a fresh energy, Claude had said, which he had clearly gained from moving to Paris. I haven't got the letter here with me, but Claude was right. It is impossible not to feel that the move had given Arp some new sense of purpose; had opened new doors, I think the phrase goes in English. Claude felt a need to share in this new inspiration, even considering following him, but bigger cities were not a healthy place for a writer such as he, especially with Anita to consider who was then working in a perfumery in Place Kléber. Do you know Place Kléber?' he asked. 'Arp had sent details to Claude of his publishing of some poems in a small pamphlet, the news making Claude envious. Even if Claude was only seconds from Gutenberg's statue – you must have seen it – the act of getting work printed and published seemed highly unlikely in the town at the time and was to prove elusive for the entirety of his life. So ironic, isn't it,' Patrice said. I began to tell him how the square was only named after the placing of the statue several hundred years later than when Gutenberg was even vaguely in the area – its previous name actually being Place de la Révolution – but it didn't matter much to the academic, whose eccentric character was beginning to come through again.

'I used to think that perhaps Arp had picked up the spirit of Goethe, who had stayed in Strasbourg for a few

years. Have you seen his bust on the building? It's *awful*
isn't it? Go and see the statue near the university instead.
Anyway, Claude,' Patrice continued, 'cursed his apartment
overlooking the river at the time, though I'm glad he never
acted upon his cursing of it!' He gave a loud, hearty laugh
again, inducing the customers of the coffee shop to turn
once more in the direction of our table, an action I was
amusingly getting used to. 'But then Hans, so my great
uncle often said, had an aura around him that suggested
that he would strive further than the rest of them, to "further
places" was the phrase he always used when discussing his
ambition, in French of course. He assumed that Arp would
embed himself in Paris permanently and follow his success
there. Yet a year later, after my uncle had been forced to take
municipal work to fund his own creative writing and to look
after his daughter, my father's cousin, Arp surprised him by
writing from a new address in Weimar. He had enlisted at
the *Kunstschule*,' he said. 'Arp suggested he was becoming
more interested in the plastic arts, though he also hinted
already at his boredom with the form in another letter.
Anything formal was beyond him, or at least an aversion
to him,' Patrice said. There was another photo on the table
of Great Uncle Claude, now older, sat with Anita and their
daughter in some grass, maybe in some quiet spot in Parc de
l'Orangerie again, though Patrice was unsure. 'My father's
cousin,' Patrice continued, 'was born Jeanne, and I think
Claude named her after Jean-Hans, well at least in part,' he
laughed. 'So, the birth of Jeanne was a great stress to Claude
as it fixed him down in Strasbourg for good and certainly did
not allow for the travels that Arp was indulging in, which
were clearly pivotal, *pivotal*, to his work.' I noticed how

tired Claude seemed in the photograph. Neither parent had bothered with the sort of stylish attire they were wearing on their other visit to Parc de l'Orangerie a few years before. Great Uncle Claude was even wearing what appeared to be shorts and seemingly could not bring himself to look at his family. It was a picture that suggested nothing except a reluctance to settle down, as if the subjugation of the energy that could have fed into work had been absolute and had literally withered the couple into ordinariness.

'Arp's time working on his practice was marked by a sense of oddness in his letters to Claude,' Patrice said, 'though they rarely spoke of little else but success. I'd have brought some of them here, but the rest of the archive is held by the university library and you know how precious they can be. In between this success, when he was writing in German at least, there was an unknown presence, I think. It's hard to describe the sense Claude attributed to it but it's definitely there in the letters that I've read personally and, if you read that volume there, Isabelle, it's in his poetry too,' he said, hinting at something unnameable and, at least for me, lost in translation. I was surprised at how dramatic he allowed himself to be in front of a total stranger. Here was an older man, talking of the potentially esoteric influence surrounding an artist, by no means well known where I was from, to somebody who could be anybody. 'Arp wrote that there was,' Patrice said, 'no logic to this presence and it beckoned him to follow, to explore its shapes. He seemed to recreate it in his work which was starting to cause great stirs in the art world, though these stirs were not always positive. His work was an attempt to try and realise this presence, if only to convince himself that it was actually there and was not some illusion of the mind. So, he began to end his letters with strange shapes which seemed almost liquid and meaningless. If you've seen his work as much as I have, Isabelle, you'd recognise these shapes. They're like this,' he said as he produced a postcard from Le Musée d'Art Moderne. It was of a piece called *Configuration*, made much later on in Arp's career, though I'd only gathered as much from a handy print of information about the piece in small type on the back. There was a flat surface standing upright upon which liquid-looking circles bled out, almost organically. From having been obsessed with following the shapes before my own closed eyes as a child, it did have something about it that suggested a natural outgrowth of something from an inner point that spread out organically from a centre. Perhaps it was the blank, impossible face of the Erl-King, rendered as well as it could be by the human eye. Abstraction was all that could protect the viewer from a dreadful truth.

'When he first did this, Claude mistook the design – for it was a design and not random – to be an accident of the pen. There was no logic to it, but that, Arp wrote later on, was the point. *Mon Dieu*, I laugh when I consider what Claude thought of such unusualness. His writing was the most formal and awful work imaginable. He writes about flowers and certainly not those *du Mal*,' Patrice said, and he let out a great laugh once more before continuing with a last gulp of his enormous coffee. '"Such formal logic"– your language makes it so difficult to translate! – "was the danger and cause of the calamity around them, forcing them out of their natural state."' Patrice didn't simply recite this but turned over the postcard in his hand to show what he had just said quoted in blue ink on the back in French. With all of this information, delivered in quick, blurry English, Patrice drawing words unnaturally together, I felt more and more lost. I had barely read any Arp and yet, here I was, learning the intricate detail of his work while sat in an American chain coffee shop. I kept thanking Strasbourg quietly in my mind as Patrice continued to talk. But my overriding feeling was still suspicion, something I couldn't shake. What had concocted this?

'Claude dared not tell him that by then he was working in a bureau, spending most of his time sorting the finances of others. At that time, Claude had accepted his poetry and writing to be a pastime, perhaps to be discovered after his death, the poor innocent. But, as a testament to Arp's work, he now lived creatively through the letters which I know he awaited with great anticipation. Claude wrote only briefly of his own progress, or lack of, in his replies, considering radical changes to its style as he thought he had little to lose. Yet there was Anita and young Jeanne, who Claude called *Petite-Jeanne*, to consider. He did not have time to experiment, to get away from the flowers. He was a failure, languishing in Baudelaire's shadow, do you follow me, Isabelle? Have you ever felt that? Being stuck somewhere, sat in the shadow of another's greatness? Poor Claude,' Patrice said with wide, passionate eyes.

I had been listening to Patrice for some time but knew that there was much more to tell. I faked a desire for another coffee, knowing from his character that it would be two that I would order in the end. He thanked me before I left for the counter. I was thinking of *Petite-Jeanne* and what became of her. Effectively she was Patrice's aunt; a temporally strange

realisation as his photos only showed her as child. In this
sort of situation, experienced myself as the daughter of a
painter, I wagered that she would have had some creative
life, perhaps even little choice in such a thing. I also thought
of another name, seen on the biography of Arp on my copy
of *La Grande Fête sans fin*: Sophie Taeuber-Arp. I had heard
her name mentioned in the discussions of Dada and had
vaguely translated the biography which suggested that she
had moved with Jean-Hans to Strasbourg when the artist
had claimed French citizenship. I carried the pair of coffees
back to the table, feeling like I was losing my sight, as if my
eyes were failing, heavy with sandstone-tiredness, before
settling down and preparing for another round of listening.
Patrice did not have much more of my time, I thought, feeling
exhausted and still wet; such a state allowing thoughts of
my father to enter. 'What about *Petite-Jeanne*?' I asked. Dr
Patrice looked up and separated the last photo from the
packet. It showed a young girl alone, stood aloof next to a
tree. 'That's her,' he said. 'She grew up to be a painter and
worked briefly in fabrics as Sophie Taeuber-Arp had done.
I haven't even mentioned Sophie Taeuber-Arp, how terrible
I am! There's little here to show you but it's worth noting
that her work is of considerable standing now, again held
in that blasted archive, arguably in just as great repute as
Arp's. Their work is often shown together, and there's even
a house she designed in Clamart. Such a shame about her
death. The records show Arp never really got over it. Gas, I
believe, and not by her own hand either. A total accident.' I
later searched and confirmed this, finding out that the artist
had died accidentally of gas poisoning while in the house
of Max Bill in Switzerland, due, so it is said, to a faulty gas

cooker. 'Sometimes,' he continued, 'I see Arp's later work almost as wisps of gas, or perhaps even the last elements of Sophie Taeuber-Arp as her spirit left her body, though I don't tell many academics that! You know how cold and stifled they can be about feelings! Easier to sneak out a holy relic from the Vatican than to show you something connected with Sophie Taeuber-Arp, though,' he laughed. 'But there is something to see that I highly recommend if you get the chance as it's close by. The pair worked on the interior of the Aubette in Place Kléber. The building is incredibly old, but their interior is as if walking around inside their work, along with Theo van Doesburg's, of course, who helped with the commission. Do you know him? Go there. I guarantee it'll be worth your time, Isabelle.' I promised that I would, having already read of the building's history in a previous spate of research, though not connecting it to something quite so modern. I told him to continue, feeling the day's hours tick on, the rain having ceased a while back.

'Arp,' Patrice said, 'spent some time in Munich before finally making the journey to Switzerland, where Claude would eventually lose contact with him. Yet, before his career took off properly, he would visit Strasbourg again to see Claude and Anita. The war was looming, and it would force a major change on Hans Arp, who would forever be Jean Arp. Switzerland provided neutrality and it seemed the logical place for him to go, especially after his successful exhibition in Zurich with Kandinsky whom, so Arp told Claude, he had become friends with by sheer luck. I don't think Claude could hide his envy towards him any longer when he told him of the many great artists he was now acquainted with, his life as the great Dadaist and everything

else. Claude would tell me of his visit when he was much
older, remembering it very well indeed; the final visit before
the move to Switzerland. He mentioned how Arp seemed
much larger than the town he was now visiting, how he
seemed to be almost constantly plagued by visitations of
something that neither he nor Anita could see. "It is there,
the split in the logic of my perception," he once said to Great
Uncle Claude. You can be proud of me translating that, all
those television programmes in English have paid off! Do
you like *Game of Thrones*, Isabelle? Anyway, I remember that
quote of his well, wrote it down in fact. He had been sending
grainy photographs of some of his sculptural work, the
fluctuating shapes and all his usual things. Claude thought
that perhaps these were the shapes he was referring to,
though what allowed him to see them was never revealed.
Petite-Jeanne was out working somewhere for most of that
visit, but I know that Claude was already worried about
her own similar visions, as if the city had given them both
something. *Petite-Jeanne* should have been a great artist but
was blinded in her mid-twenties, a terrible incident. She took
her own life, you know. Arp, now Jean, left Strasbourg and,
in the remaining handful of letters he sent from Switzerland
to Claude, made it apparent that the war would ground
him there and he would not visit again, at least to see any
of *my* relatives. Perhaps he did visit Strasbourg again –
most probably did, in fact – but I know nothing about it.
Memories of the art world reminded Claude of his failures
and I know that he died an incredibly frustrated man, empty
after the early death of his daughter too, obviously. It was
not until after the war that Arp wrote to him one final time,
well after the death of both their partners, enclosing a small

package which contained some published poetry. I'm sure Claude was glad to see that he had not entirely dismissed the poetic form. It was called *Die Wolkenpumpe* and was actually his second published collection in German from some years previous. There were many other volumes, but Claude had stopped following Arp's progress as life drifted by. This is the copy he was sent.' Patrice lifted the pamphlet on the table, revealing the little brown book to actually be the volume he was talking about. I picked it up and leafed through it, though I was more taken with the design on the front cover which, to my eyes, looked like the head of a man, covered in a sack before being hung or executed, or perhaps some shrouded figure.

'I wondered what this all meant to Great Uncle Claude, you know, Isabelle; that contrast of Jean Arp writing in the language of Hans Arp,' Patrice said. 'But, have you noticed something: that he published it simply under the name Arp. Jean and Hans were now one. When I walk down Rue du Vieux-Marché-aux-Poissons, I often look up at the house that was once his and wonder if the plaque there should be dedicated to Jean Arp or Hans Arp, rather than Jean-Hans Arp. As the years go by, the question seems less and less important, don't you think?' He picked up the old volume of poetry and riffled through it before putting it away. It looked so small and inconsequential but, with what Patrice had told me, it felt heavier knowing the sadness it probably brought to his relative. 'So,' Patrice said, 'what do you think to all that?' I wasn't sure what to say but I was glad that the conversation had happened, surprised even by the chances. I expressed my thanks to the man and asked what he planned to do for the rest of the day. He didn't know, but he did mention that he was often found in this particular coffee shop hiding from his colleagues, if I ever wanted to check something and have a general chat about Arp and art, of which his specialities were acute. He slid a small business card along the desk, which I kept. I was grateful beyond words, to him and to Strasbourg, and made to leave, putting my coat slowly over my shoulders and slipping my arms inside, feeling the shake of my hands from the caffeine. Before I said farewell, I had one last look through all the photos that Patrice had brought with him in his little archive of Arp. I was particularly fond of the first picture of Claude and Anita, sat stylishly in the park. There was something optimistic about the picture that I could not quite place, perhaps the optimism that happens before children come along. Luckily, I thought then, my partner had kept his thoughts on such matters quiet. I left Patrice in the cafe, our conversation feeling at its natural end. We said our farewells, knowing that we would probably not meet again even though he would undoubtedly still frequent the chain as usual. It was I who was moving on. 'Very nice talking to you, Isabelle. Enjoy the rest of *La Grande Fête sans fin*. I'm sure,' he said finally, 'it will have greater meaning to you now.'

I craved the more natural surroundings of my usual cafes, housed in old creaking buildings around Petite France and the university quarter, sick of the forced interior of the chain and its almost constant muzak. I would leave Patrice alone with the memories of his relative, whose connections I felt invariably envious of, if they weren't all a pack of lies. It could have been an elaborate fiction concocted for pleasures unknown by a lonely academic, but it was too elaborate, too detailed. I wandered back past Arp's house once more, noticing the people walking by below the sign, totally unaware of its presence. The clothes in the shop below seemed to draw more attention than the plaque and the little demon that sat in menacing grimace beneath the memorial. I knew exactly where I wanted to go: to the Aubette in Place Kléber that Patrice had mentioned, a building I had only visited previously for its English language bookshop underneath. It was a regular place for my partner at birthdays and Christmas, it being easier to give him a list of books I wanted which he could then give to the shop, rather than him having to think of things alone. The rain had stopped, thankfully, and so without further ado I wandered slowly up Rue du Vieux-Marché-aux-Poissons, past Gutenberg and further up Rue des Grandes-Arcades. The road was filled with people shopping, making the most of the break in the weather. There was the man with dreadlocks I sometimes saw in Petite France making large bubbles with a pair of sticks, an older man playing the violin, and another pair of musicians, one playing a single drum, the other playing some sort of woodwind instrument that I could not name. The road was alive as the buildings turned modern before opening out into the huge expanse of Place Kléber, with the general stood at roughly the centre. The Aubette took up the whole other side of the large square, the old building almost like a palace. Underneath it were several shops, including a lingerie shop and a coffee shop of the same chain I had just spent the afternoon in, the latter feeling viral in its gradual spread over the city.

The building above was adorned with commemorations to a variety of composers, chosen seemingly at random, at least to my heavy eyes. It took a while to find the official

entrance to the Aubette, finally finding the door right next
to the coffee shop, which led to a corridor. Upon the walls of
this corridor was a history of the building and then, finally,
references to Jean-Hans Arp along with Sophie Taeuber-
Arp. There was a picture of them together walking in front
of the building and it was surprising to see the artist looking
happy. He seemed so downtrodden in every other photo I
had already found of him. I walked along the wall taking in
all of the information, lost in its detail once more like being
taken underwater. The Aubette itself was the result of the
architectural theorist Jacques-François Blondel combined
with the powerful Secretary of State, Duc de Choiseul;
famous, like Gutenberg, for amassing a range of debts,
later settled by the Duc's widow, Louise Honorine Crozat
du Châtel. The building was used for military purposes,
named after the early-morning change of guard; the men
sleepily awakened and marched into the square on winter
mornings when, so I thought, the cobbled area would take
on an endless, frosty quality. Arp's relationship to the project
had already been detailed by Patrice but there were extra,
pleasing details on this wall. The Arps had worked with van
Doesburg, and the whole trio had found themselves on the
project because of the architects Paul and Andrè Horn as part
of their wider urbanisation plans. Jean-Hans had decorated
the basement bar and dance hall, while Sophie Taeuber-Arp
had decorated the tearoom and the actual Aubette bar. I was
dizzy with detail as I made my way up the stairs.

A man greeted me and instantly assumed, correctly,
that I was English. He took my driving licence from me
and put it in a small tin for safekeeping while giving me
an iPod in exchange, on which there was an audio guide

telling the history, though I was not to listen to it. I wanted the experience of it with Patrice's story in the background instead, not the official history. On the stairs, there was a great window of blue glass, dazzling the steps with oceanic qualities. At the top there were three ways to go, so I turned left into the huge function room. Its walls were rendered with geometric patterns filled in with colour, not unlike the paintings of Piet Mondrian. A security man followed me suspiciously around before taking a seat on a chair in the Cine-Dancing room. I followed the walls around, losing myself in dreams as faint 1920s dance jazz played from an unseen speaker. It had a powerful effect for the music rang hazily through the vast space, simultaneously hinting at the great amount of people who would have been in these rooms at any one time in Arp's day but also highlighting my loneliness, my virtual isolation in the building, being its only visitor. I could see a piano decorated with strange designs and colours too, and I instinctively took out the volume of Arp's poetry to read in the room.

Patrice occupied my thoughts momentarily before giving way to other, more troubling visions. I felt myself falling back, the room filling with people extravagantly dressed and drinking luxurious looking drinks. I was sat at the table alone, these people sometimes stopping to ponder my presence before they would walk on towards the dance floor, the band beginning to play a selection of standards. My father was there somewhere, perhaps trying to convince someone to buy a painting or failing in an attempt to get my mother to dance. I needed to snap out of it and so I hit my hand upon the black-painted wood of the table, the noise bringing me back to the present, where both the Arps and my father were dead. I stood up, noticing the security guard entering to check what the noise was and, doing my best to look innocent, I wandered off. He shrugged his heavy shoulders and walked back to the main foyer. I noticed the mirrors on the walls next to the windows, all of which gave views of Place Kléber and the people wandering through it. I could not help but look at myself in the mirror, looking at my tired eyes, my weary body, how my own curves which I had once admired as being attractive in a clichéd way had wasted into nothing. The eyes which had travelled through others' histories in order to not see the present, to be blind by choice, were almost hollowed to a darkened shadow. My body had been ravaged by a switch in lifestyle, by the torments and joys of a ravenous creature, desperate for the pleasures and desires of my fading being. I hated the Erl-King and his desires, not least because I had allowed them and failed to resist them. I hadn't missed his rancid caresses totally since he had failed to show in those weeks, but now all that was left was icy solitude. Perhaps I would, in those horrible moments of engulfing loneliness, seek his touch, his violent embraces, his total possession of my body which he threw around with gleeful thrusts and scratches until we shared our collection of little deaths.

Outside in the square, I saw a man I had previously seen while reading in a cafe earlier in the previous year. He was walking through the square with his two great walking sticks, both taller than him and with a V-shaped branch at the top of each one. The other people around seemed to be standing stock-still while he, to my eyes, moved slowly through a sea of statues, all melting into liquid shapes just as in Arp's vision. It must have seemed incredibly odd to the guardian of the Aubette; that someone spent much of their visit staring out of the window. The pilgrim eventually crossed the square back onto Rue des Grandes-Arcades; perhaps down to see the statue of Gutenberg, whose fortuitous invention had failed to help even this poor wanderer many centuries hence. I made to leave, to head back to Petite France and message my partner, in spite of how useless it all now felt. I wanted to work on my research on Jean-Hans Arp back at the flat, but I was again captivated by one of the mirrors on the wall which almost glowed with its reflection of the space back upon itself. I could have sworn, back in the Aubette, that somehow its polished glass was radiating something, as if having stored a blessed essence for many years behind its reflection. I stood with my back to it for some time, wondering what relic the Arps had placed in front of it many years ago. When later searching for Patrice from the information on his card, nothing would turn up. I tried and tried but there was simply nothing online. He was just another ghost, another emissary of the Erl-King, perhaps even the creature itself, I thought, taking human form to mock me with his presence, knowing how I missed his visitations. I had had enough of spirits.

A curiosity shop sits on the corner of Quai au Sable where it joins with Rue de la Râpe. On one side begin the impressive gates of the Palais Rohan, completed in 1734 to the designs of Robert de Cotte, first architect to the king, while on the other a variety of buildings sit within the shadow of the cathedral's square. The shape of the palace building lends all other structures around it a certain extravagance, the design being the famed *entre cour et jardin*, its U-shaped framing creating a terrace on its inside. Such architecture signalled the arrival of French designs after years of independence as a free city, with Louis XIV taking control of the bridge over the Rhine. In the curiosity shop, even today, there are two famed objects which connect distinctly to Strasbourg's history. The first object is highly unusual and considered rather morbid by some curators. At first glance, the object merely seems to be a section taken from the trunk of a middle-aged tree. The spirals of its wood can be seen, though the freshness has faded to a smooth darkness in the years since it was cut. On both sides of it is a thin plate of glass which connects to a wider wooden frame made out of even darker wood. This dark wood makes a very thick support which frames all the way around the large object, except for a small opening on the top which also has a tiny glass window. Looking closely, however, a small gap in the trunk can also be perceived through this window. It is difficult to tell exactly what it is at first; the space, perhaps a crack or hole in the bark, is filled with what looks to be dust. But closer inspection reveals the crushed wings and black, round eyes of what was once a species of moth, its face still just recognisable through the disintegration.

Though there is some dispute as to which exact moth it was when alive, it is clearly of a family whose caterpillars built their cocoon in small, warm gaps in trees and then emerged later on in the year. This is different, however, as the gap this poor insect chose, or perhaps made, was ill-fitting, and, due to some change in the climate, the bark shrunk towards the outer section of the gap. The wood curves inwards like the

inversion of a funnel. At some point, the moth hatched out
from its chrysalis but could only grow into the space before
its own size crushed up against the wood. The frame's
separate window allows a view onto the remains of the
moth's tiny eyes through the small gap, its face blank and
decayed but still perceivably there like a dying prisoner in
a cell. The object was supposedly found by Louis François
Élisabeth Ramond, Louis Ramond de Carbonnières as he is
sometimes known in more political recollections of history.
He was a noted botanist among many other things. Ramond
was born in the city in 1755 and went to the University of
Strasbourg in its earliest days, most probably to study law.
He was notably fond of Goethe and had become obsessed
with German Romantic literature, especially the poet's *The
Sorrows of Young Werther* which he had been introduced to
by his friend, Jakob Lenz, the writer of Romantic volumes
of *Sturm und Drang* prose. The friends had travelled into
the mountains of Switzerland, Ramond later developing an
obsession with understanding the formation of the valley
of the Rhine. He had even tried his hand at being a novelist
of Romantic leanings, and he briefly lived in Paris before
finally returning to Strasbourg to continue along other
paths. His epic novel, *The War Of Alsace During The Great
Schism Of The West Ended With The Death Of The Valiant Count
Hughes Nicknamed The Soldier Of Saint Pierre*, was published
in 1780 in Basel but had little success, not least, as has often
been suggested by scholars, because its title must have made
discussing the book a chore. Ramond became secretary to a
controversial cardinal in Strasbourg whom he accompanied
at the time, the cardinal always on the move chiefly to avoid
many scandals. The scholar became obsessed with the flora

in the more mountainous regions of the country where the cardinal sought refuge and soon parted company with him to follow his own interest in these mountains, including the peak of the South of Bigorre, which he admired greatly. He soon organised a trip to Mont Perdu in search of interesting finds and, as was fashionable in that period, he tried to reach the peak. Though his expedition failed to get to the top, items of interesting natural history were found. The segment of tree with the buried moth, now often referred to simply as the 'moth's tomb' in its English translation, came from this venture, perhaps from some tree cut for firewood.

Ramond's life was equally fruitful in politics. He refused the role as first prefect of the Hautes-Pyrénées, married the widow of General Louis-Nicolas Chérin – a woman whose hair was said to shine like silver after her first husband's death – and then eventually became the prefect of Puy de Dôme thanks to his growing friendship with Napoleon. But he seems to have been reluctant to perform his administrative duties or exercise virtually any aspect of his political power, spending more time pottering, planting and surveying the weather than helping to run the country. He seems to have become Baron of the Empire through simply planting bulbs and tracking the life of mountainous species of plants, still publishing botanical books right up until his death, when he was finally Council of the State.

The moth's tomb is considered a macabre object, itself gifted with a curse to those who handle it, though such characteristics are played down by more scholarly writers. Visitors to see the object often sit like mourners sat around a body, unsure how to react, and so silence is often asked for when visiting the shop to see the object. The second object housed in the shop is known by the locals as *La minuscule pierre tombale*. It is similar in construction to the moth's tomb and often the pair are mixed up when in discussion, as they are both likened to graves of some description. The frame of a cube is made of dark wood but with each face, except that of the base, being made of glass. The base arches out like the stabilising parts of a plinth and is covered in a soft green material underneath so that it does not slide easily when sat upon a smooth surface. Inside the display there is a large grey stone with moss covering it, so dry as to seem almost part of the stone itself. Around the stone, there are further fragments of moss, grey in death but still perceptibly there. It resembles nothing less than a diorama, conceived for some dramatic effect or recreation rather than for purely scientific reasons. However, there is a small plaque made of gold at the bottom of the display which reads '*Mousse collectée dans les montagnes du Jura par Andreas Franz Wilhelm Schimper, 1877*', which somewhat removes its dramatic qualities. Schimper was another noted botanist, son of Wilhelm Philippe Schimper, another botanist who first demarcated the Paleocene, though much later than Ramond's time. When he was born in Strasbourg it was part of Germany, though he similarly went on to study at the university before travelling around the world. He sadly caught malaria which eventually led to his demise. Before the illness took hold of his body, Schimper became Professor of Botany at the University of Basel, where he died. He is arguably best known as one of the first to argue that plants were limited by different climate areas, especially in the spread of seed-bearing plants. As many have suggested, it is Schimper we have to thank really for the demarcation of the tropical rainforest.

Though the history between these two men is connected
only by what could be called certain similarities, they came
together many years later to surprisingly influence one of
Strasbourg's most celebrated photographers, Oliver Franck,
not to be confused with Martine Franck who was also a
successful photographer and Henri Cartier-Bresson's second
wife. Franck was born in the city at some point in the very
late 1800s, and, though now overshadowed by the many
urban photographers that developed in Paris at roughly the
same time, he is considered one of the foremost landscape
photographers of the twentieth century. Franck's education
was minimal, having said to be kicked out of his school, the
Lycée International des Pontonniers, when it was simply
the Lycée Municipal, for stealing a number of minor objects.
He quickly apprenticed in one of Strasbourg's engineering
workshops where, at some unmarked point, he found a
broken camera. Later interviewed towards the end of his life in
a photographic journal, Franck said that it was the act of fixing
this old 35mm camera that led to his desire to take photographs
with it, rather than anything specifically visual that he had
in mind. This is, at least, before Franck acknowledged the
profound effect that seeing the moth's tomb in the curiosity
shop by the Palais Rohan had on him as a child. It was when
his mother, on a rare day off from the apprenticeship, insisted
on taking him to see the strange artefacts, that Franck became
interested in landscapes and, in particular, trees. He was, by
his own admission, not a scientist, but simply harboured an
interest in trees generally; something which began to assert
itself later in his photographic work. He was, of course, never
influenced by the Keller Group who, when asked about them,
knew nothing.

Franck was a loner by the city's creative standards. By his mid-twenties, having narrowly avoided the war by being too young at its start and then engineering at an important munitions factory when he was the right age, he was working as a photographer for the local paper, photographing many local businesses and people for a variety of articles. As during his schooldays, however, Franck soon became dissatisfied with the work he was producing and quit the newspaper to begin exhibiting his own photographs. It was at this point when he, in his own words, thought back to the moth's tomb connected with Louis Ramond for inspiration. Trees had held a fascination for him for many years since seeing the dead moth enclosed in the wood; trees always carrying a sense of strangeness, especially as the woods stood in stark contrast to the streets of the city. Like the phytologists before him, Franck would begin to venture out of Strasbourg in search of woodland to photograph. 'Winter was the best time,' he once said, 'because the light and the trees arguably work together.' Franck conducted many interviews once his name became known, the artist dubbed the 'Cartier-Bresson of wood and branch'. Yet no picture exists of the man, having never photographed himself and always profusely refusing to be photographed at any time, even when interviewed. 'My face is in my work, it's in those trees and the way the light shines through their branches,' he said in his very last interview before he died in 1978.

Franck's workmanlike approach to his practice also meant there was little organisation to it, and certainly nothing like the Keller Group of artists whom his work is unfairly considered an evolution of. Many photos are considered lost,

especially from his days as a photojournalist, as the building of the paper he worked for was bombed during a raid in the Second World War. Franck survived that war despite actively taking part in the fighting, rumoured to be a member of the resistance acting in the Bas-Rhin area during the years of the occupation. 'The forests took on a different approach after those years,' he once said. 'They helped us in so many ways; they were cover, they hid our tracks, they provided us with fuel, they virtually looked after us when camped out and on the run.' Many conversations with the photographer often devolved into this sort of anthropomorphism, imbuing trees and forests with human qualities gifted with disturbing believability. His earliest surviving photo is from the extensive series *Les Bois*, a selection of forest portraits taken in the cold winter of 1934. The forest, said to be further north of Strasbourg, is covered in snow, and the stunning winter light that shines through the picture meant that it was noticed early on by photography critics. 'I imagined,' Franck once suggested, 'that all such trees had these trapped moths within them, just like Ramond's piece of trunk. All trees had dead eyes looking out and I suppose there's a nervousness to such pictures, at least for me. It was like walking around a peaceful but vigilant graveyard.'

Following in the footsteps of Ramond and, to a lesser extent, Schimper, Franck ventured further into the mountainous regions of the area, determined to capture taller trees and to base his compositions around their great height. He stopped photographing people entirely and focused on trees and forests instead. Some critics have considered this to be why he is overshadowed by most other French photographers

from the period, as the vogue was explicitly to capture people and their lives. 'Landscape was for painters if for anyone at all, not for people like me. I was expected to shoot people drinking in cafes and dogs jumping in the air after cats, not trees and woodland.' In a paper entitled 'The Eyes of Trees', the art historian Lucia Wilson has suggested that Franck's visual style was more in line with those early street photographers but is often unfairly gauged solely on the subject matter. 'His trees stare back towards the viewer just as much as any city dweller stares back towards Cartier-Bresson's lens. It is our own inability to see what Franck sees in his pictures that has muddied readings of them, virtually since the earliest reviews of his work.' Wilson is one of a number of academics and critics to make this point, but is the only one to suggest that such indentations and markings on the bark of the trees in question act, in the most literal sense, as eyes that stalk the viewer and the photographer.

Franck would mention the influence of the objects from the curiosity shop only a handful of times, usually referring only to the moth's tomb rather than Schimper's little grave, though he undoubtedly saw both on his early visit. Appropriately, in his last interview, he paid his respects to the moth's tomb, as already suggested, but he went further. 'You know,' he said to interviewer, Carlos Bellini, 'I sometimes wonder whether I didn't end up like that moth.' When asked what he meant, he merely said that the wood had enclosed around him; a sort of metaphor for how his interest in the trees had led to his work being largely disregarded, marginalised and only of interest to a very specialist audience rather than ordinary people. 'I wouldn't mind being buried in the nice big trunk

of a tree though. Not a coffin, but a tree, hollowed out and put into the earth.' His wish was granted in early 1979 when, after a short battle with cancer, Franck was entombed in the hollowed-out trunk of a large tree felled near Normandy. He was buried in this wooden tomb, like that of Ramond's moth, under the soil of his favourite forest of the Bas-Rhin in an unmarked grave, 'guarded by his true audience,' as one critic wrote later in their obituary of the man.

The flow of the Ill had often taken me in its current. I had spent so long wandering along its banks and along the cobbled paths away from Petite France that I had rarely explored the local vicinity of my partner's flat by Square des Moulins. It overlooked the picturesque Ponts Couverts where, in the height of summer, flowers on some of the older buildings turned the architecture into a trellis of stone and colourful buds, especially upon one particular house that sat right in the centre and was supposedly the clinic of a private psychiatrist. Summer was still far away, and my winter exile had felt incredibly long, avoiding England and death through the solace of Strasbourg's streets and its demons. It had been an irresponsible thing to do as my stability eroded, and yet it had felt like my only option, if only to avoid the past reigniting. Spring was slowly approaching, and I felt my body equally finding a new life of sorts. I had been struck by a deathly frost and was only beginning to warm back to life once again, away from hanging bodies and deathly shrouds. The Erl-King was threatened by the warmer weather – unusually warm, in fact, as February turned to March. He had stopped his haunting of the streets, the flash of movement at my sides, the nightly, forlorn visits using me for his pleasures. I was notably alone, with messages now only coming from the department with increased desperation as to when I would be back. I knew they'd let me go on my arrival after such eccentric behaviour, so I felt little rush to return. My mother had stopped trying, as had my partner, though I was convinced the latter had concluded our relationship through his silence and was merely hoping I would drift out of his apartment and leave it tidy for when he returned later in Spring. The sun was shining in a way that it had not done for months since my father had died but the air still felt cold with the breeze, as if winter was reluctant to fully and finally relinquish its clinging grasp. I was not to follow the river that day but instead decided to cross it directly, filing all of my research papers and postcards in neat piles on the table between the medical books before making my way out of the flat. There was enough amassed for a book; perhaps my career could be saved after all. I refused to follow the water any longer, to fall into conversations of the sort that had swept me along all those months in the city, especially since talking with Dr Patrice, who had been impossible to find anything about since, as if the city had created him for that one afternoon and disassembled him after I had left. I had spoken to enough people and knew that there was more to life than this endless tunnel of grief.

The Ponts Couverts and their defensive designs were built in Petite France in the early 1200s. But parallel to this bridge was another strange building that similarly crossed the river and was more modern, at least by the area's architectural standards. The water ran underneath this building through gaps with metal bars hanging down, while the stone walls rose two storeys before its textured rooftop revealed a path often walked by tourists. The building was the Barrage Vauban, built in the late 1600s as a defensive proposition, later put to use in 1870 against the Prussians in the Franco-Prussian war. The stonework of the Great Lock, or the *grande écluse*, was made of Vosges sandstone, rendered a pinkish amber in certain lights on winter mornings. As soon as I had noticed this building, I began researching its history in between gazes out of the window towards its rooftop. All it had ever recalled for me was seeing a police boat drag the body of a teenager out of the water; a drunken accident that had provided a brief spectacle for confused tourists before they continued to photograph the architecture. The building was designed by a flamboyant military engineer for Louis XIV called Sébastien Le Prestre de Vauban, who drew up the designs on parchments of velum and had a propensity, perhaps even an obsession, so an article insinuated, for the defensive potential of zigzag designs. He was not a native of Strasbourg but an outsider from Burgundy, orphaned but soon successful, with many engineering feats completed during his lifetime. I felt a slight affection for the man when reading about him in a printed pamphlet from one of the museums, largely because of his interest in siege warfare. I was a living embodiment of his plans, trying my utmost not to let the intruder of emotional fallout gain the walls by zigzagging my responsibilities. Vauban's defensive design was a final transposition of my own emotional projections.

On the other side of the Barrage Vauban, I imagined England and the corpse of my father rather than armies of Prussians. I later learned, after walking through the lock, that Vauban had left the designs in the hands of another

engineer, a fellow colleague, Jacques Tarade, whose
name adorned the road further up the river, Rue Tarade,
appropriately adjacent to Stade Vauban where a variety of
small sporting events were held over the summer. Today,
Tarade and Vauban still sit side by side. I had heard of
Vauban on my first walk through the lock but only knew
of the story of his body. Like Frédéric Chopin and Kléber,
he seems to have been separated from his heart; a situation
I felt keenly in rhythm with, as if I had torn out my own or
someone else had at the least done the job for me, imagining
the Erl-King coaxing me into humiliating blackmail with my
beating organ held in his slender, outstretched hands. The
mob had opened Vauban's grave during the revolution in
Paris and peppered his body all around into the oblivion
of the streets. It was only in the early 1800s that his heart
was somehow found and reinstated in Les Invalides by
Napoleon. Some weeks previous, I had found a postcard of
Napoleon in the pocket of a jacket in a second-hand clothes
shop on Grand'Rue. It was unusual to me then, as now,
because the postcard was written in English, far older than
the jacket it was folded into. The letter writer complained of
terrible weather and appalling delays to trains, among other
trivialities. I had not bought the jacket at the time, though
had secretly pocketed the postcard and slipped out of the
shop, avoiding the expensive old clothes that probably
would have been compulsory to purchase in order to obtain
the postcard had I asked. I found it an alluring object, coffee-
coloured with the passing of time and showing Napoleon as
a child. Such pictures often suggest that these men of war
had some essence of perceivable power even as children –
straight-faced, cold, ready to decide the fates of thousands

while barely old enough to drink wine – but, as in most cases, all I could see was a child who seemed, at most, deathly unhappy. I used the postcard as a bookmark, rendering its edges haggard after mere days, as it was then lodged hastily in page 206 of the English translation of Zola's *La Terre*, which filled most of the left pocket of my jacket on that day when I finally walked through the Barrage Vauban, determined to finish the book soon. I was glad to be able to read it finally, having avoided it beforehand due to Zola's links to Crystal Palace, where he was exiled for a time. I now felt I could continue with a reading that had started in late summer but had halted abruptly for obvious reasons.

There is a contrast with Barrage Vauban created by the new building behind it, the building I was heading towards that day. In the Barrage, the path was uneven, while the view on either side was not of the water but instead a variety of marble statues suspiciously caged as if they might awaken and wander around after nightfall if left free to roam. Cobwebs hung heavy on these statues and I was unable to rid myself of the feeling that we were one and the same. I was encased in amber. I had sunk into Strasbourg as an act of self-defence but had been trapped in the process. Once I learned of the existence of these statues – some of men, some of animals – they preoccupied my mind whenever I stared out of the window of the flat. The building was, after all, one of the main views from the window of Rue du Cygne. It had always been a surreal sight to see tourists wandering on its roof, sometimes sitting dangerously on its sloping design in warmer weather to take in the hot Strasbourg sun. With the season slowly turning, some had already begun to do this, but, as I watched them from the window, their bottle had given out due to the

persistent breeze still maintaining winter's spirit. The side of
the river that it led to had always felt uncomfortable, hinting
at potential trains back to Strasbourg-Entzheim Airport or
Basel through Colmar and, ergo, flights back to Stansted
and London. The thought always produced a shudder in my
lower back as if my spine was threatening, of its own accord,
to collapse if such a possibility was entertained. I would
rather fall of my own accord, like my father had done, than be
besieged totally by England once more.

I paid my dues to the dusty statues, and came out on the
other side of the building. It opened out onto a large square
where water spouted from certain panels in the pavement
in summer and which, due to its open space and interesting
modern architecture, skateboarders made regular use
of, jumping and grinding across things. They were often
the only people there, the sound of their wooden boards
grinding along the cheap stone acting like grace notes over
the general melody of the water flowing by. After this visit
in my final days in the city, I would sometimes sit and watch
them attempt their tricks and jumps, but on this occasion I
wanted to enter the building behind them: Le Musée d'Art
Moderne. I had not visited the gallery until the late days
of my time in Strasbourg, which was partly an avoidance
of sorts. It contained a number of works by Jean-Hans Arp,
among others, but the thought of seeing paintings had been
tainted in those months. I had retreated into journal entries
and streets but had, for some reason, avoided most art as
it reminded me too deeply of my father. I could picture his
paint pots and primed easels still lying on the desk in his
room, though I had not seen it properly for a while by that
point. I could just see my mother, going through it all, taking

great pleasure in stuffing it all in black bin bags.

I was determined to break out of this winter. I had heard, or perhaps had seen as a poster on one of the cafe walls, that there was a retrospective of the artist Gustave Doré in the gallery. Doré was born in Strasbourg and connected with all the other figures I felt I had met; a genuine local who had used art to fall into light and shade. I was to go against the flow with Doré's help. His work would finally perhaps mark the conclusion of my grief. His art had seemed so prescient to the city, almost haunted by it. When on a bus to a spa the year before with my partner, before he went travelling to South America, I noticed a small board inside the bus on which one of Doré's illustrations was proudly displayed along with a small history of the artist and his relationship to the city. It was a basic illustration by his standards, made up of primitive stickmen, and it was to my surprise when finally getting off the bus near the spa that I noticed Doré's stickmen blown-up to huge proportions and emblazoned on the side of the bus too. The day of my conversations with Dr Patrice regarding Jean-Hans Arp was, in hindsight, actually Doré's birthday. He was born in January, on the sixth. This information raced through my mind, the coping mechanism, a self-induced amnesia of objects and facts all hiding one solitary truth that I would still not face fully. Doré's life seemed far more light-hearted in tone than my mood on the day I went to see his work. His days as a youthful prankster in Strasbourg eventually earned him work illustrating the *Le Petit Journal pour rire* in Paris by the time he was a teenager. But the seriousness of his later work was what had lured me, even if the men hobbling and etched onto the side of that bus by the spa were mostly comic. I could still picture the

overweight man running with his arms raised as if fleeing
from something, several keys strangely thrown in the air
and about to fall to the ground like dead leaves.

The sun reflected off the glass of Le Musée d'Art Moderne
and created vibrant kaleidoscopes on the ground due to
its multicoloured windowpanes. As I entered its small
courtyard, where a security door closed behind me, I noticed
that the square itself was also named after Jean-Hans Arp; his
name imprinted upon the city. Like most galleries of this sort,
it was vast and filled with only a handful of works on display,
though it probably housed many thousands of works of art in
its vaults. Paying a few euros to enter, I tried to void all of my
thoughts, if only to refuse the link that many of the pictures
created to my father and England. Even paintings by Picasso
and a sculpture by Rodin could not help but remind me of
my country sinking slowly under the waves, along with
the hanged corpse of my father which swung in the forest
where he had lost all sense of choice. I considered the Rodin
sculpture, if only due to its size and its title – *Le Penseur*, or
The Thinker – though this was, as I later found out, a facsimile
and obviously not the original. *The Thinker* was supposedly
Dante, whose book *The Divine Comedy* was the inspiration for
Rodin's series of sculptures; destined in the physical world
to be tormented, but perhaps briefly able to transcend such
pain and sorrow. The walls of the gallery, like so many of this
kind, were white and gleaming, and I imagined them to be
of a similar ilk to the mortuary or resting home where my
father was probably held before he was buried, burned and
scattered. I needed to stop thinking of my father.

Perhaps my mother had kept his ashes in that harridan
way of hers for purposes unknown; it wouldn't have

surprised me. I had since gone through my mother's messages methodically, accepting that I had been irresponsible in my avoidance but also enjoying the minor revenge for years of her abuses. I had, however, yet to build on my one reply to her since she had broken the news of his death. 'These thoughts *must* stop,' I told myself out loud; a realisation that only occurred when I heard the natural echoing reverb of the space added to my own voice. It was when entering the room designated as the start of Doré's retrospective that the ill feeling that had crept up on me began to diminish. The amnesia of history was working once again. I could drown in information and my death would be a calm moment, an ochre sleep. The room was not white but painted a deep red. The pictures were much older than anything I had seen in the other rooms, and felt locked off from the period in which I could associate with the calamities of England. *The Divine Comedy* was present once more: two onlookers staring into Hell's gate, a rocky precipice with unseen fires and rancid smoke bellowing from somewhere ominously below. It was a breathtaking picture. Who were the two watching on? I could not recall ever reading Dante's poem and could not place the two figures. I imagined standing there next to my father; were we going in together? Or had we avoided this? We were both atheists but the worry over Hell had especially troubled me after his death. Did he really trade his small studio in Crystal Palace for an eternity in that spiral? Grief does strange and terrible things to the mind; rationality disintegrates into the air. I wandered further, following the walls and the main etchings of Doré, focussing intensely on the details of the ink, the lines and the shadows. I knew, however, that I was only here to see one picture, so much so that I had researched its presence before bothering to walk through the Barrage Vauban and pay the entry fee. The history of the picture had obsessed me since first seeing it as a teenager.

In the 1860s, the Matterhorn – the most famous mountain in Zermatt on the Italian-Switzerland border – had sat unclaimed by climbers. Edward Whymper, a sporting man hired to provide illustrations of the Swiss Alps, later developed an obsession with climbing to the peak of the mountain. After several years of attempts and failures, a party of eight led by Whymper climbed to the top. Such was the popularity of defeating the mountain at the time, Whymper and his associate, Michel Croz – the French mountain guide, forever with a curved pipe protruding from his mouth and an ever-growing long beard – gave word to a rival party, led by Jean-Antoine Carrel, further down the mountain via the throwing of stones down the cliff to show that they had reached the summit first. Carrel must have been frustrated for he turned back, though his fate was not undeserved, having deceived Whymper regarding his withdrawal from the climbing party, citing a booking with a well-to-do family when in reality helping his own rival group led jointly by Felice Giordano and Quintino Sella. The adventure of Whymper's expedition was documented by Doré but the one detail I found most interesting was the descent; where the climb down after the triumph had gone horrifically wrong, several members falling to their deaths onto the ice plains. Doré sketched this moment when one of their party slipped and, thanks to the safety rope that all of the men were attached to, several fell away. The rope snapped, leaving only half of the party alive and clinging to the rock face. The bodies of only three of the four missing men were ever found, the fourth having been taken by the ice of the mountain. I recalled my only trip to Zermatt, a romantic weekend from another failed relationship several years previous where the small Swiss village was dominated by winter sports enthusiasts. In spite of there being many paths around the town and other draws besides skiing, the town, with its clichéd chalets and small mountain-train, had stuck in my mind's eye, even from just a brief stay with limited exploring.

The Matterhorn stares. The whole of the town cannot help but feel at the mercy of this mountain and so, when seeing a plaque commemorating Edward Whymper, and eating fondue in a restaurant named after the climber, his story had since fascinated me. The success of the first conquest of the mountain was unusual, with the tragedy in the descent rather than the ascent. Did the ascent truly count if death awaited half the party on the way back down? Was the resentment caused by a distant relationship to my father, the man who had put his painting before all else, even his own family, now itself undermined by his death? Should I have mourned him, seen him buried, turned to ash, scattered, given my shoulder to my crying mother? I could not miss him. *You were always heartless.* Doré called his drawing *The Matterhorn Disaster*, an early documented occasion of a mountaineering accident that dimmed the excitement for dangerous mountain climbing that had become fashionable during the period. *You were always worthless.* Along with the bodies of the falling men, their optimism fell too; humanity's optimism that it could somehow reign over the whole of the

environment. *You were always a death penalty for us both.* It
was a moment of humbling that the Western world was not
quite prepared for at the height of its imperial and colonial
arrogance. *You were nothing but a burden.* In an edition of *The
Times*, one Reverend Arthur G. Butler defended the party's
dangerous ambition in a verse poem, which read:

> *We were not what we are*
> *Without that other fiery element —*
> *The love, the thirst for venture, and the scorn*
> *That aught should be too great for mortal powers.*

Doré's small illustration hung on the wall between two
differing responses to John Milton's *Paradise Lost*, and yet
The Matterhorn Disaster was far more haunting. The image
of a group of chiefly British climbers falling onto rocks
held some power over my mind. I knew this would be the
case, hence my research of the picture's presence, but I had
underestimated its power. There was a sense of hopelessness
to it that I had misconstrued. I expected mere melancholy,
a further reflection in which to drown. I had not mourned;
I had ignored all such action through distraction. I thought
of the last body on the mountain still lying somewhere,
preserved by the cold and the ice. When in Zermatt, I did
not know of this missing man, of Lord Francis Douglas of
Edinburgh. But after I found out about his story, I dreamed of
his body several times, preserved in the ice exactly as it was
with the exception of the horrific injuries undoubtedly caused
by the sharp alpine rocks. I could see this torn body under
the ice, making out the frayed skin now fixed permanently
into its new folds and tears. The dream was unnerving even

before my father had died; it had failed to recur since his actual demise. Lady Gertrude Georgiana Douglas, Francis's sister, often dreamt of finding her brother's body but it would never come to pass. She must have felt the stasis of mourning with no closure; that her brother was, physically as well as spiritually, failing to age past eighteen while her own body grew, matured and withered up until the age of fifty-one. One man on the expedition even came upon a design for several ropes and organising systems in which to attempt to rescue the lone body in the early days of the accident, but the idea petered out with the recovery of the other three bodies by a group of climbers in the days that followed. Douglas was to stay on the mountain. Doré captured it all in that moment of illustration: the loss of hope, the reality of risk, the impending fall. One man's mistake dragged the rest down; threatening their lives on the sheer, jagged walls of the staring mountain.

I felt transfixed in Le Musée d'Art Moderne, as if my feet had been impaled to the ground with nails, perhaps made of clear, sharp ice. I faded in and out of the drawing, sometimes feeling cold and mistaking it for the extreme cold of the air rushing by as the bodies, my body too perhaps, fell towards the rocks. I was only brought out of this thought by considerations of where Doré had actually lived in Strasbourg. Was it nearby? I had never walked to his house, which was number seven on the road named after him, Rue Gustave Doré. It was now a road with several boutiques and new-builds and, supposedly, a plaque that told of the artist who had lived there, made of grey stone and gilded with gold writing. I took my phone out covertly from my pocket, for pictures were not allowed in the gallery, and searched for the location of the road. I found an image of the plaque which I noticed had gone to great pains to show that Doré had lived in Strasbourg as an infant, my search even bringing up a picture of the house as it was earlier, crinkled and analogue in a photograph. Like Arp, the hint was that the city had profoundly affected the artist and had been carried with him after his departure, even if their travels took them to Switzerland or Paris, even if they died in places other than Strasbourg and were interred far from its orange-hued terraces and squares.

The streets were now mapped over my skin more than I had ever felt before, visibly rising on my flesh – a feeling I wish I had savoured, considering the thoughts that would later possess me that day – and Doré was the final connection to make. By completing the map, I could forget my own being totally through my new memories of the people I had met and the people they had spoken of. Perhaps that would be the time to return to London, protected by my own absence of self. Rue Gustave Doré was mere minutes from the gallery according to my digital map and so, leaving his artwork behind, I ventured to the road where he had lived. The sun felt brighter and warmer in the open sections of the gallery, the dark red hues of the Doré room having created a wintery illusion that was easy to fall under the spell of. The glass created a greenhouse effect and the sudden drop in temperature outside provided a small jolt. I had memorised the route to the road and noted thankfully that it was on the other side of the river once more, this time on the south side of the Canal du Faux-Rempart. The square, with its noisy skateboarders, took me to Rue Sainte-Marguerite and past L'École Nationale d'Administration where the current president apparently learnt his ways, as my partner had often proudly told me. The river rushed underneath the bridge and a tourist boat full of staring faces sat in the special compartment of the river, where it waited for the lock to fill to the appropriate height, avoiding the adjacent rapids. On the right, I looked in the window of Librairie Au Coin Littéraire, a bookshop with walls of philosophy mixed with pulp novels, translations of Raymond Chandler, family Bibles, old manuscripts, books on Voltaire and, on a previous visit, a boxed volume of the poetry of Jacques Prévert which I bought for my partner. I had even once spoken with the owner when asking about a paperback volume of Man Ray's photographs he had placed in a turning display stand in the porch of the shop.

My perception had been so closed to the outside world that I had quite forgotten how much I missed my partner, how I missed buying him volumes of Jacques Prévert that he would never read, and how grateful I was for his flat in Rue du Cygne. But it was not really him that I missed, but the people we both were before my father's death, even with our problems. In the coming weeks he would no doubt be back with a thousand stories to tell, with a thousand people to tell of and a thousand reasons to want to return to South America. But I wondered whether he would recognise the person awaiting him on his return from South America – if I ever came back to Strasbourg at all, that is. I could match his stories, I thought, as I followed the river along Quai Turckheim, with the stories of Brice, Dr Patrice and *grand-maman*; the stories of the streets and houses and buildings and chalets and stones that I had reconstructed my body and mind from. I was not mourning, I was petrifying. Stone cannot mourn.

I turned right onto Place Saint-Pierre-le-Vieux and noticed the Tabac on the left called Le Chat de L'île, so named because of a piece of graffiti by the French artist, Monsieur Chat. The yellow cat grinned with sharp white teeth out of a huge window which was taken up entirely by the artwork, as well as several smaller depictions of cats including one that looked like *grand-maman*'s ginger tom. Monsieur Chat, or M. Chat as he is sometimes abbreviated to, reminded me of the French filmmaker Chris Marker who used the cat as a symbol in one of his films alongside his own cat-symbol: an orange, stripy tabby. I loved this filmmaker's work. M. Chat haunts Paris's walls and buildings in particular and even adorns the house in Rue Courat where Marker lived and worked until his death. The artist depicted both cats upon the concrete wall as a permanent reminder of the loss. Rue Courat was just behind Le Cimetière du Père-Lachaise, the same cemetery where Gustave Doré was now buried in a modest low-level grave with a rim that allowed admirers to place potted plants, small coins and tokens of affection upon it until the weather caused sufficient damage for the grave-keeper to remove them, as if the collective grief had formed a literal, garish slush upon the grave. On my last visit to the cemetery, however, I could not find Doré's grave, the map, covered in an awkward plastic sheath as protection, instead leading me to the resting place of Marcel Proust, upon whose grave someone had left a half-used lipstick, a postcard depicting an interior by Degas where a man watched on as a woman seemed to sob half-undressed in a chair, and a selection of pens neatly put into a small pot with a design of blue painted flowers adorning its sides. I decided to wander into the shop, looking for a new lighter, my previous one having failed to light my cigarette. I stood in the small queue as people bought brightly coloured scratch-cards, individual cans of beer and newspapers, trying to recall the correct gender for a lighter; *un briquet, une briquet,* opting for a neutral, muffled 'Umh' sound to hide my uncertainty. The women behind the till went to her left and picked out the nearest lighter, blurting out the charge and handing me the blue plastic container after I had put a euro onto the counter. I didn't leave the shop straightaway, however, as the textures of the sweet wrappers, endless magazines and cans of drink had a hypnotic effect. My eye was drawn quickly to some of the sweets; something had caught my attention inadvertently. I didn't want any of the chocolate or other things that lay innocuously in garishly bright packets, but something was drawing me closer. I stared at each type of chocolate bar and sweet, moving on to the larger items; tins and bigger packets of chocolates designed as gifts, probably given as an apology or an unimaginative Christmas gift. And then I saw it.

It was a long bar of Swiss chocolate, its strange shape standing out in comparison to the other chocolate. The box was a cream colour, but it wasn't any of these factors that drew me to it, but the logo; that of a mountain depicted in dark orange, colouring the rock, while the main colour of the box filled in the potential snow. I knew without a doubt that the logo was the Matterhorn of Zermatt. This is absurd, I remember thinking. I went back to the counter and bought the chocolate, knowing that I was not going to eat it. Leaving, I tore the main packaging that had the Matterhorn on it from the rest of the box and folded it into my pocket while stood outside the shop, keeping it as a sort of strange memento; I would later go back to the gallery and buy a proper postcard too. A passer-by caught me in the act of doing this and, so I

thought, perhaps misconstrued my action as suspicious, as
if there was the possibility that I had stolen the large bar of
chocolate. I continued walking, unsure of what to do with
the rest of the bar, carrying it in my hand just as many of the
people around me were carrying fresh bread and bags. The
small, perhaps forgotten, Church of Saint-Pierre-le-Vieux
was on my right as I walked down Rue du Vingt-Deux
Novembre. I could not think of what I had gained from such
wandering, such synchronicities, all acknowledged and
locked into the buildings around, ready to be activated at
any moment by my walking within their vicinity. *You killed
him, Isabelle.* This was all quite useless now; it was all just
words. What if there were mistakes in my research too? I
had struggled with official archives online; perhaps all of
my work was riddled with embarrassing errors.

This was my history, even with its potential mistakes.
I had read and learned for so long, seeking the stories of
strangers and the past, that I had somehow seeped into the
city and the city had seeped into me. Walking along the street,
I noticed Michel, the homeless drunk who I usually saw and
spoke to on Grand'Rue. He must have been moved from the
main street and was now sat bunkered down in the arches
of a bank on the road. He spotted me and stood up to greet
me in his usual theatrical way; almost bowing but lifting his
leather trilby, inferring a desire for me to drop a euro or two
inside. He still had his speakers playing metal music loudly
and was wearing his usual clothing of metal-band T-shirt,
leather waistcoat and torn jeans, as well as his propped-up
cardboard sign: '*1 euro pour une BOISSON!*' I thought about
his little notebook, full of tiny scribbled lyrics, kept in secret
like a precious Gutenberg Bible. We spoke in English, and

I gave him some spare change before making to walk on, wishing him well in his day's begging. However, I realised that I was still carrying the chocolate and so asked if he wanted it, recalling when I had given him the *kugelhopf* before Christmas. Michel's face lit up and he took the chocolate happily, sitting down to eat it with his can of beer, failing to notice the missing mountain from the side of the packet. Every vulnerable man is my father, I thought. As he ate, I asked him about his wonderful book of lyrics, but his face turned to sadness at its mention. 'It was lost,' he said, 'when the police moved me on from Grand'Rue. A friend picked it up, but it was thrown away with my things. I think,' he continued, 'that they just picked it all up and threw it in the bin. They were emptied before I could get back, but I plan to start a new one soon!' I promised to buy him a new notebook to begin his runic scrawling again when we next met, but feigned having pressing business and said I had to go, leaving him eating the awkwardly-shaped pieces of chocolate.

Eventually, I found myself on Rue Gustave Doré, turning left to find the road only a minute from where Michel was begging. It was hard to picture Doré living there, for most of the buildings had been replaced with modern new-builds, flat concrete rising up to the sky, interspersed occasionally by large panels of glass. Number eleven still seemed an old building with its wooden door and what looked to be a stone cherub standing above the window. With it being an old building and this being a busier part of the town, there were defensive bars across it made of black metal. Attempting to find Doré's house had been pointless. The plaque that I had seen on my phone was lost, perhaps placed somewhere that I could not find or was not even here at all, while the house itself had obviously been demolished some time ago. What was I doing trying to connect these things together? The disjoint between the old world and this world was too much to bear, now feeling as if I belonged more to the former while rubbing up against the latter in a grating paradox. Where was I to go after this? The roads around had all been explored in my time here and I knew my territory perfectly. I stood on the corner opposite the cinema, which was advertising a season of Luis Buñuel films, and wondered what to do. In hindsight I must have looked odd, standing still and staring, staring like the Matterhorn down onto the small town. In the distance, geographically and temporally, an eccentric man fell to a rocky grave though it was the mistake of his group, their own arrogance in going it alone with a mere flimsy safety rope to stop their fall.

Looking further up the road I noticed the very tip of Strasbourg's cathedral appearing over the other buildings. I had always orientated myself to the cathedral, its dark and detailed spire often visible when stood in the long roads of the city. I had only ever been into the cathedral once in a fleeting moment of exploration with my partner, and it had haunted my walks ever since. I had resisted revisiting it up to this point, almost developing an aversion to it in those earlier months, as if the funeral of my father would automatically start up if I entered such a building. It virtually shadowed Rue du Vieux-Marché-aux-Poissons where I had spent so much time obsessing over the links with Gutenberg, Goethe and the Arps. I had researched the cathedral briefly on some of my earliest days after my father had died, its history being detailed enough to keep my mind on track during those first few weeks. It was now the only thing I felt I had left to see. I followed the road for quite a while, the clouds beginning to darken overhead indicating a rain shower soon approaching. I carried on through Place Kléber, several tents hiding book dealers and poster sellers. I could not help but detach myself from the journey towards the cathedral to look once more at the many white spines and volumes that I would probably struggle to read if purchased. Back up the road, turning right eventually towards Gutenberg again, the rumbling of the car park could be felt underfoot. I saw the statue once more and the cafe where I first learned of the news regarding my father, as well as where I eventually ended up talking to Brice about the tribulations of the printer in his brief time in the city. I hadn't seen the seller since, though I had missed most of the fairs in between. And then I turned onto the small Rue Mercière, seemingly designed in its tight and narrow spacing to accentuate the height and imposing nature of the cathedral more than anything else. On my left, there was an Italian ice-cream shop, on my right a man selling tourist trinkets while wearing an umbrella-shaped hat that bore the yellow stars of the European Union. The whole of the street layout – *don't think about Father* – was designed to draw your attention totally and completely to the building, even though all of the buildings around it were intricately designed with stained glass, beams of old wood, battered white shutters and detailed street lamps hanging down to provide a warm glow. Even the cobbles themselves fanned out in a forward fashion that pointed the way to the cathedral, rather like an unconscious arrow on the floor directing lost wanderers.

There was a strange tale of folklore surrounding the cathedral itself that I had read somewhere. The Virgin, during the calamitous battle with the ancestors of Charlemagne, had visited to help the city in its time of strife; a vision of her with arms outstretched paving the way to victory in battle. The cathedral was named after her to further protect its streets from future harm and malice. At that point, the cathedral was not where my interest lay. Instead, the huge astronomical clock that famously resided in its far right-hand corner was what I wanted to see. A postcard of its image would be the last I would purchase later on, keeping all of them in a small pile but one that I could not bring myself to spread out and look at again. They would sit in the corner of the flat, almost as a visual anxiety diary for my wintertime in Strasbourg and my walks. I wondered, while taking in the cathedral in Place de la Cathédrale, whether Doré had ever illustrated it. The building had the same busy detail that his illustrations possessed, seemingly endless in the textured lines and minutiae that, when seen from further away, built into one compressible whole; a cathedral made of stone in God's name or the gates of Hell opening up as two lost spectators watched on. Perhaps the cathedral was made in the same vein as *The Matterhorn Disaster*. Both the building and the mountain possessed that quality of imposing their will. It would be there long after we had all left.

The queue to enter was slow and meandering, as well as surprisingly dense considering it was still early morning on a weekday and not at a particularly busy time of year. I thought of a picture I had seen in a museum, showing the wreckage of war in the 1800s where almost all of the buildings which led up to the cathedral were in ruins. Again, there were two onlookers; perhaps they were the same wanderers from Doré's etching of Hell's entrance, seen after they had stepped through the passage in the rock. The picture was taken in 1870 after over a month of siege during the Franco-Prussian War. Strasbourg was merely strategic at that point, which had rendered my viewing of the photo with a sense of frustration; that the strategy very clearly considered razing the city to the ground. The ruins were almost too painful to look at, imagining the many bodies mangled like Lord Douglas's after he had fallen from the mountain. I thought about the destruction of all, the destruction that I had last year promised to apply to myself. 'I will destroy through history,' I had said to myself when sat on Gutenberg's statue after finding out about my father's suicide, his body hanging sodden from that tree in Crystal Palace Park.

And yet the cathedral was still standing, amidst all of that destruction, almost rebelliously. Even in the faded light of the picture, the building and its sandstone design was standing confidently. It was the same stone used to build the Barrage Vauban, the Vosges sandstone that gave it its light, orange glow when in sunlight but, as was happening while waiting to enter, darkened to a brown whenever wet. The rain had finally arrived in the few minutes before the queue meandered past the steel barrier and into the huge front entrance. Looking up, I could see – *your father perhaps, no?* – the stone turn darker with the drops of water falling onto the building. There was a sign on the doorway that I had failed to notice last time, declaring silence in every conceivable language. It reminded me of a trip to Sacré-Cœur not long after I had spent the morning failing to find Doré in Père Lachaise. That church had also asked for silence, though the low hum of people had similarly persisted. I had found it annoying and so had wandered further away from the tourist district after this to the Montmartre Cemetery, where I later found Zola's grave, a copper bust of the man since textured with many decades of exposure to the weather.

As with my last visit to the cathedral, I was amused by a recording which sounded like an official announcement through several installed speakers. The voice announced 'Ladies and Gentlemen' in several languages, as if preparing for some important notice, before the denouement of a man's voice simply going 'Shh!' With the natural reverb created by the building's height and size, it was a doubly surreal experience and one that caught several tourists off guard, expecting a gift but receiving a disciplining. The room was soon reduced to a more obvious level of silence after this first rendition of the recording. By the second time, people weren't so easily duped into submission. I wandered further inside, deeper into the darkness of the hall that I had spent so long reading about. It was an incredibly dark space in spite of the many windows and their light streaming through the glass but, with the heavy design and dark colours, it did little to properly illuminate the pews. Light from the many candles, lit in prayer and thoughts for loved ones at the small cost of a few euros, were generally the main provider of light and also a grateful source of heat in the still icy building on winter days. I knew roughly where the clock was, having researched it many months before in a state of manic reading, and so I meandered slowly through the crowd to the far right of the hall. A man bustled against me by accident and apologised quietly but I didn't mind his touch at that point of my solitude. I longed for touch, feeling frozen in a block of ice, even strangely nostalgic for the malevolent pawing of the Erl-King. The sound of people's shuffling feet pervaded, as did the slowness that came with such a movement caused by most eyes being drawn upwards to the vast designs of sandstone gospel above. I wondered if people were awed by this building still or whether it was simply another tick upon their list of things to see. I was guilty of that too, of course. The crowd seemed to die down as I approached the clock, the mechanism taking up the whole of the back wall in the square of space dedicated to the contraption. My father would have liked this, I thought. Such was the splendid nature of its design, its intricate array of gild-work, and its imposing size, the clock had regularly summoned to its shadows viewers with a more complicated desire than simply knowing the time. I felt unusually alone then, empty once again just like that first day in Place Gutenberg. Even with the handful of people moving behind me – leaving after realising that there were still some minutes to wait before a particular hour when the clock would animate itself with movement and sound – I felt like a ghost that lingered on.

The clock was of the three kings, the first actual clock being built on the site in the mid-1300s, then ceasing to function some 200 years later. This first clock, one of the earliest public clocks to be installed, must have drawn many gatherers, rather like the people who were shuffling while in awe of the other parts of the building today, taking secretive photographs on small digital cameras and phones. In an attempt to rectify the disrepair that the clock fell into, another dial was added, one which was designed to show the movements of the moon and the sun through the Zodiac; a mechanism itself worked by the general clockwork ingenuity still installed in the huge body of the timepiece. However, due to the basis of its measurements on the Julian method for its calendar, the clock in one sense had never been anything less than astronomically redundant. Work was planned for the restoration of this first clock, the role foisted upon an eminent mathematician Chretien Herlin in the 1600s, who undertook the work to entirely restructure it, hiring Dr Michel Herr, a respected clockmaker, and others to help on the practical matters of the restoration. The architect, Bernard Nonnenmacher, began work on the new casing, and the old astronomical dials and artefacts were now separated and kept in the Musée des Arts Décoratifs today, which I had vague memories of seeing but not acknowledging as being connected with the clock or cathedral. It was like finding the bone of a dinosaur before knowing what the whole of the reptile would have looked like; there was no proportion or context to seeing these things without knowing how they sat. Nonnenmacher built the spiral staircase that rose adjacent to the clock and which gave it its grand scale, but the project fell apart with the church's shift back to Catholicism. It lay as a shell for several centuries, luckily saved as an interest by its extravagant designs, its wonderful colours and the many sculptures and artworks that adorned the device. Perhaps even its sense of useless function created a haunting in the cathedral, implying a movement that was never to come no matter how hard the devoted watched on.

In the 1830s, Jean-Baptiste Schwilgué wandered into the cathedral just as I had done, only, with his work and experience as an engineer, he had instantly set to work on the renovation of the clock. It was in the later years of his life and yet the vigour of the clock's existing potential seemed to take hold of him, as one paper suggested. I imagined, as the minutes ticked by, what he would have said when first seeing the lifeless shell of the object. He added new designs to the entirety of the casing, built instruments to carve wood more accurately in order to construct the models and sculptures to fit into his automata. He even suggested an entirely new design for the clock with modern alterations and suggestions as to its design. But Schwilgué had the public and its purse against him, and so he was restricted to simply renovating and adding to the original shell and casing of the previous clock. Suffice to say, the engineer worked wonders with the design, adding turrets in which certain weights descended as part of the overall mechanism. I later sought pictures of the man and only found a handful of illustrations, also learning that the astronomical clock was the last of the engineer's creations to still live on in full working order. He seemed a calm man from the main sketch of him and certainly younger than the man he probably was when, at the age of sixty-one, he began his last great work on Strasbourg's public clock.

I haunted the shadows, the wonderful stained-glass windows behind providing a multicolour backdrop like a two-tier dream. The hour was approaching, the ticking having begun to give way to a small tinkling sound. The figures at the top of the clock began to move and it was only in that moment that I noticed death standing above me. It was he who was making the ringing, hitting with his scythe the small bell that stood next to him. Then more figurines began to move. What looked to be a cherub, moved awkwardly past death on the turning mechanism almost at the very top of the structure, then slowly followed by a much older but still youthful man, now openly dressed in Roman clothing. I could see his bow and arrow and his bronze amour. The clock was aging the man to death at only a slightly quicker rate to those who watched on from below. And then the adult was revealed by the mechanism, the full Roman soldier with his black beard and sword, and then, from later seeing a detailed postcard of the sculptures, a tired and weary face as his body was dragged in finality past death before the small chime and the mechanism fell back into dreaming; a whole life in miniature, hellishly repeating. Other tourists looked on, our time slipping away as we watched the version of life playing out above us while death chimed his bell in synchronicity. The last chime rang, and the stilted movement of death's bony arm then held still, his skull still frozen in a grimacing glare, waiting for the next marker when he would replay the ghastly absurdity of the man's life all over again. I was mesmerised by this figure of death, the sculpture possessing a manic, horrific quality. It reminded me of another of Doré's illustrations, the series he had done to coincide with Edgar Allan Poe's *The Raven*; somewhat appropriate considering later that day I wandered to the other end of the road to Place du Corbeau, where I ate and drank in Le Corbeau, a cafe accentuated by decorating the walls with prints of Tippi Hedren in Alfred Hitchcock's *The Birds*.

When the creators first designed the astronomical clock, the idea was that time could be measured in a number of ways. In fact, all of the ways conceivable were to be contained and expressed in the mechanism. Even if it was wrong, measured through obsolete ways and methods, rather like my research, the thought was there. Now, with its lunar globe – the round, black sphere seemingly made of cursed obsidian – its planetary dial and other facets, the clock seemed to fulfil this proposal and yet, by measuring out all of time in a variety of ways, all that could be gained from it was not the exactitude of its information but what this information implied: the end, the rotting end in which all perished, all entered Dante's gates, all fell from the Matterhorn, all were hanging from trees in Crystal Palace Park. I had read earlier of a legend from when the first clock was built, and that with its splendour it had caused great harm to the original designer and engineer. Such was its exquisite and unique nature in the world when first built that the magistrate of the town, fearing its reproduction in other cities by the same creator (and possibly removing its prestige from Strasbourg), had the designer's eyes slashed, leaving him blind and incapable of reproducing the work elsewhere. It was while considering this gruesome possibility that I felt my phone vibrate in my pocket. Perhaps it was my partner, guilt-ridden about his recent silence; or perhaps it was my harridan mother, sending another request to return a call or even return back to England, both after a period of silence. But, from a glance, I could swear that it was neither of them. It was from my father. Sometimes his messages had been delayed when I was visiting here, even for months, his phone being old and slow in sending things abroad as if his words were lost in digital purgatory. I thought it could perhaps be my mother playing a cruel joke, inhabiting the digital ghost of the man she had hated to spite the daughter whom she loathed, in her own harridan way, even more. I put the phone quickly back in my pocket before pulling it out sharply again and checking properly what it said. Perhaps it was not my father, or an old message coming through from months previous, glimpsed but ignored. I needed to look at it again in case he was alive, in case this had been some incomprehensible mistake which I was totally unaware of. It was easier to imagine his body hanging from a tree in Crystal Palace Park, failed as a painter, rather than face the equal reality that it was England that had died in my blind eyes, not him. I pulled it out again, my hands shaking. It was from him; delayed for months, I assumed, by a technical quirk. 'Love you Isabelle,' it said.

It was then that the Erl-King came to visit for a final time. I knew he was there and had been following me that day, but I did not face him. I felt him descend from the high roof of the cathedral like a giant spider; his movements rendered a slow glide as if harnessed by a web, drifting through the air as if it were liquid. I heard the soft sound of his shroud descending onto the stone floor directly behind me, and I closed my eyes. I could feel his breathing, the spindly fingers of his terrible hands wrapping themselves over my shoulders, as if he was ready to devour me there and then. But instead he was ready to leave; he had taken from me what he had wanted, that which he wanted from all of those he followed and whispered sweet violence to. His bony hand slipped from my shoulder and then he was gone; the excited, fearful feeling of his presence dropping away like the chime of the clock, echoing and then extinct, the moment dead.

I could feel my country many miles away slowly sinking into the abyss as my quiet tears fell onto the stone floor. I had mourned through the tramping of pavements, through conversations with the elderly, through strange and wonderful objects and the history of Strasbourg. I wanted to die, for my body to follow my mind in finality towards darkness along with the Erl-King on his journey back through the void, feeling that there was no more that I could know or learn. There were no streets upon my arms really, just a collection of red scars and lines on a thin-looking layer of skin, so white as to almost seem translucent. The clock began to tick, or at least its ticking seeped into my consciousness like sap from my father's hanging tree, the amber creaking into stony existence in between the crevices of my thoughts. Sunlight leaked through the large, thin windows of the cathedral directly above the mechanism. The rain shower that had arrived during my walk to the cathedral must have subsided, for the threatening sun now shone brightly. The warmth of its light reminded me of the many months I had stayed there, the calamities that seemed to be occurring all around like a receding tide meeting incoming water and creating a whirlpool that could only be avoided by staying in Strasbourg. Yet I had never felt less mapped; the streets and buildings were not etched upon me, the rows of houses were not flowing through my veins, and the cathedral, with its astronomical clock, was not embedded in the centre of my heart like a stake. It was all gone.

I felt weak and alone, my partner never seeming further away than at this moment, my mother and my father afterthoughts. It was all fading. The light shone upon my right arm, illuminating the bare skin revealed by a rolled-up sleeve, irradiated by a variety of colours from each piece of coloured glasswork. I looked down, feeling the ground, perhaps even the whole continent, slip away beneath me. My homeland over the sea, a fatherland of sorts, was sinking as I clung on desperately to France, to Strasbourg and its astronomical clock. I was being dragged down with my

country, even from a distance. My skin was white from many
months without sun and warmth. I would undoubtedly
burn when the incredible warmth of the city's summer
burst again into its streets, and I would be blind once more
when my partner returned from South America, if he would
still be my partner at all. The clock's mechanisms whirred
in the background as I stared at my arm, considering the
deathliness of my skin beneath the season's dying light.
How pale the winter has made us, I thought.

'I shall never know if that warmth, that sweetness, did not emanate simply from deep within me, the last efforts of a man struggling against solitude and the cold of the night. But the question, which arises also in the presence of our living loves, has ceased to interest me now; it matters little to me whether the phantoms whom I evoke come from the limbo of my memory or from that of another world.'

— Marguerite Yourcenar, *Memoirs of Hadrian*

Acknowledgements

This book came about due to my visits to the city of Strasbourg and so I must first and foremost thank the people of the city, in particular Caroline, and the friends I've made and met during my visits, all of whom have made me feel very welcome over the last few years.

With working in cafes, I could not have found a more inspiring setting to write in, and so my thanks for the generous hospitality of the staff at Café Bretelles and Coffee Stub in particular who have put up for hours with a frowning British man slumped in the corner trying to write. I must also thank the wonderful street sellers of Strasbourg in helping me find so many evocative photographs which became so integral to the process of writing.

Considering the sheer numbers of edits this book has gone through, all for the better, I must thank Gary Budden and Dan Coxon who were very patient with me as the book changed dramatically from week to week. My thanks as ever to Gary, Kit Caless and Sanya Semakula at Influx who continue to support me in an industry that I still struggle to deal with. Thanks as well to Vince Haig for his beautiful design work.

Lastly, thanks as always to my parents Keith and Janet who continue to support and guide me in ways I think even they are unconscious of.

INFLUX
PRESS

Influx Press is an independent publisher based in London, committed to publishing innovative and challenging literature from across the UK and beyond. Formed in 2012, we have published titles ranging from award-nominated fiction debuts and site-specific anthologies to squatting memoirs and radical poetry.

www.influxpress.com
@Influxpress

MOTHLIGHT
Adam Scovell

'An eerily compelling book reminiscent of Arthur Machen, in which the self dissolves into the flapping of flimsy wings.'
— Luke Turner, author of *Out of the Woods*

'The idea was lost but the memory was there.'

Phyllis Ewans, a prominent researcher in Lepidoptera and a keen walker, has died of old age. Thomas, a much younger fellow researcher of moths first met Phyllis when he was a child. He became her carer and companion, having rekindled her acquaintance in later life.

Increasingly possessed by thoughts that he somehow actually is Phyllis Ewans, and unable to rid himself of the feeling that she is haunting him, Thomas must discover her secrets through her many possessions and photographs, before he is lost permanently in a labyrinth of memories long past.

Steeped in dusty melancholy and analogue shadows, MOTHLIGHT is an uncanny story of grief, memory and the price of obsession.

ISBN: 9781910312377

CAR PARK LIFE
Gareth E. Rees

'A retail park *Heart of Darkness*.'
— John Grindrod, author of *Outskirts*

'Compelling, insightful and teeming with mid-life spirit.'
— Andrew Kötting

Car parks: commonplace urban landscapes, little-explored and rarely featured in art and music, yet they shape the aesthetics of our towns and cities. Hotspots for crime, rage and sexual deviancy; a blind spot in which activities go unnoticed. Skateboarding, car stunts, drug dealing, dogging, murder

Gareth E. Rees believes that the retail car park has as much mystery, magic and terror as any mountain, meadow or wood. He's out to prove it by walking the car parks of Britain, journeying across the country from Plymouth to Edinburgh, much to the horror of his family, friends – and, most of all – himself. He finds Sir Francis Drake outside B&Q, standing stones in a retail park, and a dead body beside Sainsbury's.

In this darkly satirical work of non-fiction, Gareth E. Rees presents a troubling vision of Brexit Britain through a common space we know far less about than we think

ISBN: 9781910312 353

BUILT ON SAND
Paul Scraton

'With a psychogeographer's sensibility and a deep connection to history, Paul Scraton's *Built on Sand* offers us a tender, fresh, and moving portrait of Berlin.'
— Saskia Vogel, author of *Submission*

Berlin: long-celebrated as a city of artists and outcasts, but also a city of teachers and construction workers. A place of tourists and refugees, and the m emories of those exiled and expelled. A city named after marshland; if you dig a hole, you'll soon hit sand.

Built on Sand centres on the personal geographies of place, and how memory and history live on in the individual and collective imagination. Stories of landscapes and a city both real and imagined; stories of exile and trauma, mythology and folklore; of how the past shapes and distorts our understanding of the present in an age of individualism, gentrification and the rising threat of nativism and far-right populism.

This novel offers a portrait of a city three decades on from the fall of the Berlin Wall, and the legacy of that history in a city that was once divided but remains fractured and fragmented.

ISBN: 9781910312339

EXERCISES IN CONTROL
Annabel Banks

'Occasionally absurd, often disturbing, so much of these stories' essence lies in what is left unsaid. Elusive, quietly accumulating moments of unease are expertly woven into everyday situations using exquisite imagery and sparse prose. Banks's voice is versatile yet distinctive, with sparkling touches of dark humour set against an ever-present lingering sinister shadow.'
— Lucie McKnight Hardy, author of *Water Shall Refuse Them*

'We do have a complaints procedure. You will find paper and a pen (chained) to the shelf by the bin. Write your concerns and then place them in the bin. PLEASE NOTE: We do not allow items to be placed in the bin. Please do not write on the paper.'

A lonely woman invites danger between tedious dates; a station guard plays a bloody game of heads-or-tails; an office cleaner sneaks into a forbidden room hiding grim secrets.

Compelling and provocative, Annabel Banks's debut short fiction collection draws deeply upon the human need to be in control – no matter how devastating the cost.

ISBN: 9781910312476

Lifetime supporters: Bob West and Barbara Richards